Sophie Winthrop Weitzel

# Sister and Saint

A sketch of the life of Jacqueline Pascal

Sophie Winthrop Weitzel

**Sister and Saint**
*A sketch of the life of Jacqueline Pascal*

ISBN/EAN: 9783337313548

Printed in Europe, USA, Canada, Australia, Japan

Cover: Foto ©Andreas Hilbeck / pixelio.de

More available books at **www.hansebooks.com**

# A SKETCH

OF THE LIFE OF

# JACQUELINE PASCAL.

BY

## SOPHY WINTHROP WEITZEL.

NEW YORK:

ANSON D. F. RANDOLPH & COMPANY,

900 BROADWAY, CORNER 20TH STREET.

# CONTENTS.


### CHAPTER I.

A Home in Auvergne, - - - - - - - - 3

### CHAPTER II.

Poetry and Geometry, - - - - - - - 15

### CHAPTER III.

The Cardinal frowns; the Cardinal smiles, - - 29

### CHAPTER IV.

Into Normandy, - - - - - - - - 41

### CHAPTER V.

A Flemish Bishop, - - - - - - - - 55

### CHAPTER VI.

The Director of Consciences, - - - - - 65

### CHAPTER VII.

"The Obstacle becomes the Instrument," - - - 79

### CHAPTER VIII.

A Happy Year, - - - - - - - - 95

### CHAPTER IX.

Climbing, - - - - - - - - - 113

### CHAPTER X.
Port Royal and the Mére Angélique, - - - 133

### CHAPTER XI.
At the Convent Gates, - - - - - - - 151

### CHAPTER XII.
Waiting, - - - - - - - - - - 167

### CHAPTER XIII.
The Lord Opens the Way, - - - - - - 189

### CHAPTER XIV.
Fresh Trials, - - - - - - - - - 205

### CHAPTER XV.
A Bundle of Letters, - - - - - - - 221

### CHAPTER XVI.
Teaching the Convent School, - - - - - 239

### CHAPTER XVII.
The Masterpiece and the Miracle, - - - - 253

### CHAPTER XVIII.
Sorrowful Days, - - - - - - - - 275

### CHAPTER XIX.
Those Left Behind, - - - - - - - - 295

### CHAPTER XX.
(Supplementary). Fragments gathered up, - - 309

# INTRODUCTORY NOTE.

As good Bishop Jansen's ponderous book is said to have been "a tissue of texts from St. Augustine," so the web of this brief biography is woven of many threads from various authorities.

Much of it is translation, some portions are adapted from previous translations. Every important item has been verified by reference to the best sources, especially to Sainte-Beuve, the acknowledged chief of Port Royal historians. Thus, though slight, the little history claims to be accurate. Its only aim is to lead to further acquaintance with the books on which it is founded and the noble group of characters it introduces.

The following authorities may be consulted with profit and pleasure by any intelligent reader:

## FRENCH.

Jacqueline Pascal. Premières études sur les femmes illustrés de XVIIe siècle. *V. Cousin.*

La jeunesse de Madame de Longueville. *V. Cousin.*

Mme. de Longueville pendant la Fronde. *V. Cousin.*

Vie de Jacqueline Pascal par Mme. Perier, sa sœur.

Vie de Blaise Pascal par Mme. Perier, sa sœur.

Lettres, opuscules et mémoires de Gilberte et de Jacqueline, sœurs de Pascal. *Faugère.*

Mémoires de Marguerite Perier sur sa famille. Scènes d'histoire et de famille. *Mme. De Witt, née Guizot.*

## ENGLISH.

Select Memoirs of Port Royal. 2 vols. By M. A. Schimmelpenninck.

Life of Angélique Arnauld. By Frances Martin,

Life of Pascal, by Principal Tulloch.

The other books to which I refer will be chiefly interesting to those who are making a special study of the subject.

Port Royal. Par C. A. Sainte-Beuve. 7 vols.

Mémoires pour servir à l'histoire de Port Royal. Par M. Fontaine.

Mémoires touchant la Vie de M. de St. Cyran. Par Lancelot.

Vies intéressantes et édifiantes des Religieuses de Port Royal.

Faugère's introduction to *Pensées de Pascal.*

Leben Jacqueline Pascal. Nonne von Port Royal. Dr. Reuchlin.

I mention also a Life of Jacqueline Pascal, published by Carter & Brothers, 1854, from which I have taken some translations of poems.

*June,* 1880.                                        S. W. W.

Great hearts alone understand how much glory there is in being good.

MICHELET.

# A HOME IN AUVERGNE

# I.

## A HOME IN AUVERGNE.

HISTORY gives us some charming glimpses. A distant city, a cluster of village dwellings, perhaps a solitary abbey catches the mind's eye, just as in a hasty journey roofs peep out here and there beneath which we would gladly linger, or a ruin flashes on us for an instant whose story we wish we could stop to hear.

A wonderful picturesque charm gathers about certain names of places—it is the charm of vivid circumstance, of dramatic event, of lofty character— all this under the enchantment of distance in time and difference in manners.

Whenever we hear these names, though we may have little actual knowledge of the history connected with them, a picture rises to the eye and an interest stirs in the mind.

Clermont, in the province of Auvergne, just south of the heart of sunny France, is one of these names.

The very word is breezy and suggestive. And from
all we can learn of the surrounding country—mount-
ainous and bold, yet rich and smiling—it seems fully
to merit the affectionate praise with which Jacqueline
Pascal celebrates it in these lines:

> " A climate, fertile in unnumbered charms,
>    Though ornaments, save Nature's, it has none;
>    In stern simplicity, untouched by art,
>    It yields a picture of its Maker's power.
>    There,—in Auvergne,—from those proud peaks afar,
>    Whose gloomy heights nor fruit nor harvests know,
>    But in their stead dark precipices yawn—
>    Rises a little hill, so fresh and fair,
>    So favored by the Sun's celestial ray,
>    That *Clairmont* seems its most appropriate name."

Our first glimpse of Clermont is an exceedingly
striking one. Thither in 1095 came the pope, Urban
II., with a great retinue of bishops, priests, and car-
dinals, to hold a solemn council and preach the first
crusade.

Mellowed but not dimmed by the far mediæval
light, we see the picture;—the broad open *Place*
before the already noble cathedral, densely packed
with a swaying, shouting, excited, expectant multitude
—Rembrandt-like old men leaning on their staves,
oddly-dressed women holding aloft oddly-dressed ba-
bies, pious, humble peasants from the remotest hamlets
of the province, come up to look once, before they die,
on the representative of their Lord upon the earth,
and to receive from him a blessing.

Gay silken banners and festoons of gorgeous *arras* adorn the tall, steep-gabled houses that front the square. Ladies and children in costume the most brilliant and *bizarre* appear at the quaint, small, unglazed windows.

White hands (oh, how long ago turned to dust!) wave greetings answered by the gleam of knightly helmets in the square below.

In the distance is heard the stirring sound of trumpets, then the solemn chants of the Church. Then slowly comes into view the long procession of priestly dignitaries. Last of all, the pope himself, seated on a white mule, solemnly advances through the now hushed and kneeling multitude. He is conducted up the carpeted platform prepared for him, and pointed to the throne. But he turns his back upon it. His message can not wait. "Il fait un geste de grande impatience," says the old chronicler, and turns toward the people.

Then follow those burning words which, kindling on this ready populace—springing from low to high, from high back again to low—seizing with equal violence ignorant peasant boys and girls and the great Count Raymond of Toulouse with Elvira, his beautiful wife—spread from this center over all France, from France over all Europe, and resulted in the sublime madness of the crusades.

As the pope's voice ceased, it is said, a solemn cry

burst from the multitude, "It is the will of God! It is the will of God!"

A knight tore in pieces his scarlet mantle, and pinning the bits together in the form of a cross, fixed them on the shoulders of those near him. The crowd pressed eagerly around him to obtain the fragments. The booths of the merchants surrounding the *Place* were entered and rifled of their scarlet stuffs, and soon the inspiring emblem blazed on every side.

A few weeks later the fountain plashed to a silent and deserted square. The knights were gone. The ladies and children lingered no longer at the windows in holiday attire, and we shall never again see Clermont in so picturesque a light as on that November afternoon.

Six centuries after this we know of Clermont, or rather of its overhanging mountain, Puy-de-Dôme, as one of the centers of scientific experiment on the weight of the atmosphere, of which experiments the barometer is the result.

Again we read of the finding of the *codex claromontanus*—an early copy of St. Paul's epistles—in the monastery on the side of the mountain. This is a manuscript highly valued by scholars, and Tischendorf published it in fac-simile not many years ago.

To-day Clermont is a noisy, humdrum, manufacturing city. A railway connects it with Paris, but terminates here, so that the city stands, as of old, portal and fortress to the wild, rich province of Auvergne. It is quite out of the way of tourists, and even the "commercial traveler," intent on his purchases of linen or woolen fabrics, hosiery or paper, scarcely lingers long enough in the old *Place* to feel its quaint, peculiar charm.

To us, in this little book, Clermont will be chiefly interesting as the early home of the Pascals.

In the city's best days perhaps—the early part of the seventeenth century—this family lived here. The father, Etienne (or *anglicé* Stephen), was President of the Court of Excise. This was a high-position, open to him as member of a wealthy and influential family of long standing in the province. It had not been a titled race till, in 1478, Louis XI., in recognition of faithful service, bestowed upon it that honor, and thus our friends became possessed of that best patent of nobility which comes of good works.

They lived, of course, in some stateliness—this father and his little family of one son and two daughters—yet in much less than our modern American notions of elegance would lead us to suppose. For nowhere is the simplicity of true dignity more conspicuous than in the daily life of the high families of France. The furnishing of those lofty, airy rooms, the quiet *ménage* and simple diet would surprise us by their plainness.

The eldest daughter, Gilberte, was obliged early to

"look well to the ways of her household," for her mother died when she was but seven years old. But while practicing her various domestic arts and learning that delicate craft of cookery in which every French lady is trained, she was not idle mentally. Her father taught her history, Latin, and mathematics, and with such success that she is mentioned by her brother's biographers as "une femme très-instruite." She became a vigorous thinker—and in those days there was a deal of profound and practical thinking to be done —and in the specimens of her writing left to us in sketches of her brother and sister, her style is remarkably clear, graceful, and pleasing.

Blaise, the son, came next to Gilberte on the family record, and then the little Jacqueline, born in 1625, and a baby of a year old when her mother died. Blaise is the central figure of this family group. But for him we should have known next to nothing of Jacqueline, and nothing, probably, of Gilberte and their father.

Blaise Pascal was first a thinker, then a saint. A wonderful combination of scientific acuteness and child-like faith, a shining example of great mental and great spiritual qualities, and one whose name will be always honored by men as diverse as the materialist and the mystic.

We could easily linger over his story. But seen in the side lights of family life, perhaps we shall

find him quite as interesting as if more directly studied.

And, indeed, so intimate is his kinship with his sister Jacqueline, so closely interwoven the web of their deepest experiences, that, in reading of her, we must of necessity come very near him.

This brother and sister were only about two years separated in age. They were companions in study and in play. His thoughts were her thoughts, not only in childhood, but throughout life, and so great was their sympathy in all respects that they have been spoken of as " spiritual twins." Her mind in youth was more versatile than his, and, while climbing with him to all his heights, she carried with her a feminine lightness and charm, " to cheat the toil and cheer the way," which must have been invaluable to him.

Both these sisters, Gilberte and Jacqueline, are said to have been " parfaitement belles," which is certainly strong language." Gilberte, as soon as she was old enough, mingled in society suited to her rank, and was much admired, being beautiful, graceful, and very witty. And when Jacqueline, six years younger than Gilberte, in her turn grew to womanhood, her charms were not unrecognized, as we shall see.

And now, from this home in Clermont, let us look out for a moment over France and over Europe, and

1*

see what kind of a world it is in which the Pascals pass their childhood.

On the throne of France sits Louis XIII. But on the throne behind the throne, ruling with a rod of iron over king and people, is Richelieu, prime minister and cardinal. Just at this time he is building for himself a new house—the *Palais Royal.* The large court-yard of this palace, now surrounded by brilliant shops and cafés, is familiar to every American who visits Paris. Almost everybody has taken a cup of coffee under the horse-chestnut trees, and bought a bit of clever imitation jewelry in one of the arcades. This is all that is left to-day of the glory of Richelieu's residence. The spacious halls and galleries, which extended in all directions from this central court, have more than once suffered from violence and fire since his time.

At the time of which we write, the Reformation had taken thorough hold of Germany, and Protestants in France had become so numerous and powerful as to be worthy of Richelieu's hatred. His wars against them, and against England, as friendly to French Protestantism, came to a successful end in 1628, when Jacqueline Pascal was three years old.

Louis XIII.'s queen was Anne of Austria. She seems to have been chiefly remarkable for two personal peculiarities. One of these was an exceedingly delicate sense of feeling in all parts of the surface of her body, so that all ordinary linen and cambric was rough to her, and it was exceedingly difficult to find fabrics fine enough for her use. How fortunate that she was a queen, and not a peasant woman, doomed to die of homespun!

Her other distinguishing peculiarity was such an aversion to roses that she could not even look upon a painted one.

Altogether she seems an uninteresting, indeed rather a disagreeable woman, and we do not much wonder that her husband was content to live the greater part of their married life in complete separation from her.

Louis himself was a respectable and honest man, and that is saying a good deal for a king. He was not fond of ruling, and, indeed, had little chance for it, but he was full of bravery and self-possession in war, and much honored and admired by the soldiery. His morals were not corrupt, and for purity and true nobility his court was a happy contrast to that of his more brilliant son, Louis XIV. When, after twenty-two years of married life, this son and heir was born, there was the greatest rejoicing throughout the kingdom.

Thus matters stood in France. Across the Channel Charles I. was on the throne, and Archbishop Laud endeavoring to act in England something corresponding to the part which Richelieu was acting in France.

The Puritans were stirring. Every day they grew more powerful, and were soon to break into open rebellion. Already some had left the country, for as we well know, the *Mayflower* had anchored off Plymouth Rock in 1620, five years before Jacqueline Pascal was born.

There were no daily newspapers in those days. But we may well believe that the table-talk of an intelligent family like the Pascals would now and then fall upon these themes. Their father would, perhaps, tell them some fresh report from the Dutch colony at New Amsterdam, or the English in Massachusetts or Virginia, or their own French settlements in Louisiana. They were faithful little Catholics and all Puritan proceedings would be sure to strike them with abhorrence, but we can imagine their delight, nevertheless, in some of the strange, wild stories, and altogether it must have been an interesting world out at which they looked from their quiet home in Clermont.

# POETRY AND GEOMETRY.

# II.

## POETRY AND GEOMETRY.

WE have a record of Jacqueline's early years in Gilberte's little book, entitled "A Sketch of the Life of Sister Jacqueline de Sainte Euphémie, by birth Jacqueline Pascal."

"I was six years older than she," says the writer, "and can remember that as soon as she began to speak, she gave signs of great intelligence, besides being very beautiful and of a kindly and sweet temper, the most winning in the world. She was, therefore, as much loved and caressed as a child could possibly be. At seven years old she began to learn to read, and, by my father's wish, I became her teacher. This was a troublesome task, on account of her great aversion to it, and do what I would, I could not coax her to come and say her lesson. One day, however, I chanced to be reading poetry aloud, and the rhythm pleased her so much that she said to me: ' If you want me to read, teach me out of a verse-book, and I

will say my lesson as often as you like.' This surprised
me, for I did not think that a child of her age could
distinguish verse from prose. I did as she wished,
and after that time she was always talking about
verses, and learned many by heart, for she had an
excellent memory. She wanted to know the rules of
poetry, and at eight years old, before knowing how
to read, she began to compose lines that were really
not bad."

Before this time the family had moved to Paris.
In 1631, when Jacqueline was six years old, Blaise
eight, and Gilberte twelve, their father made this
change of residence on account of the greater facilities
for education in the capital. Since the death of his
wife he had considered himself especially responsible
for the rearing of his children, and devoted himself to
them with almost a mother's tenderness. He taught
them not only language, science, and *belles lettres*, but
grounded them thoroughly and systematically in religious truth, as he understood it. His son's education he took entirely into his own hands, Pascal never
entering any college or having any other master than
his father.

In order to attend thus particularly to his children,
Etienne Pascal was obliged to give up business, and
on leaving Clermont he sold his office of President of
the Excise Court, and invested largely in stocks of
the *Hotel de Ville* in Paris, one of Cardinal Riche-

lieu's speculations. He did not, however, give up his house and other property in Clermont, and the family returned occasionally to their native place.

In Paris the children entered at once upon a pleasant and busy life.

Gilberte says of Jacqueline at this time, "She was so pretty a child, and so agreeable, that she became a general favorite, in request with all our friends, and spent but little of her time at home.

"She had, in particular, two playmates who contributed not a little to her enjoyment. They were the daughters of Madame de Saintot, and themselves made verses, though not much older than Jacqueline; so that in the year 1636, when my father took me with him on a journey to Auvergne, and Madame de Saintot begged that she might keep my sister with her while we were gone, the three little girls took it into their heads to act a play, and composed plot and verses, without the least aid from any one else. It was, however, a coherent piece, and had five acts, divided by scenes regularly arranged. They performed it themselves twice, with some other actors whom they invited, before a large company. Everybody wondered that such children should be capable of constructing a complete work, and many pretty things were discovered in it, so that it became the talk of all Paris for a long time."

The story goes on, and though we may suspect it

of a little pardonable sisterly partiality, it is so fresh and natural that we can but quote :

" My sister continued to make verses about anything that came into her head, as well as on all extraordinary occurrences.

" When the Queen was expecting an heir, she did not fail to write on so fine a subject, and these verses were better than any of her previous efforts. We lived at that time very near Monsieur and Madame de Morangis (a gentleman and lady of the court), who took so much delight in the child's pretty ways that she was with them nearly every day.

" Madame de Morangis, charmed with the idea of Jacqueline's having written verses on the Queen's situation, said that she would take her to St. Germain and present her. She kept her word, and on their arrival, the queen being at the moment engaged, every one surrounded the little girl, in order to question her and see her verses."

Jacqueline was so small and so simple in her ways that the ladies felt a little suspicious as to her being the actual author of the lines. Mademoiselle de Montpensier, niece of the king, then a young girl, afterward " the great Mademoiselle," was one of the company.

" If you can make verses so well," she said to Jacqueline, " make some for me."

The little girl went quietly into a corner and wrote

the following, evidently composed on the spur of the moment :

> " It is our noble princess' will,
>   That thou, my Muse, exert thy skill
>   To celebrate her charms to-day :
>   Hopeless our task !—the only way
>   To praise her well is to avow
>   The simple truth—we know not how ! "

" Now make one for Madame de Hautefort," said Mademoiselle, and Jacqueline in a few minutes read them this impromptu effort :

> " Oh, marvel not, bright masterpiece of earth,
>   At the prompt tribute by your charms called forth.
>   Your glance that roves the world around
>   In every clime hath captives found.
>   That ray which charms my youthful heart,
>   May well arouse my fancy's art."

The child, we see, has already caught the courtly trick of flattery, and the lines, to us, seemed stilted and artificial. But we must remember that they are French poetry, and French poetry of the seventeenth century as well as the production of a little girl.

" Soon after this incident," goes on Gilberte's story, " permission was given to enter the queen's apartment, and Madame de Morangis led my sister in. The Queen was surprised at her poetry, but fancied at first that it was either not her own, or that she had been greatly aided. All present thought the same, but Mademoiselle removed their doubts by showing them the two epigrams that Jacqueline had just made in her presence and by her own orders. This circumstance increased the general admiration, and from that day forward my sister was often at court, and much caressed by the King, the Queen, Mademoiselle, and all who saw her. She even had the honor of waiting on her Majesty when she dined in private, Mademoiselle taking the place of chief butler."

Jacqueline was not the only member of the family admitted to the presence of the great. Soon after they came to Paris, M. Pascal had taken all his children to see the cardinal. Cousin tells us of this interview that " Richelieu's eagle glance at once selected these children from among the waiting crowd in his audience-chamber. Struck with their remarkable youthful beauty, he did not wait for the father to introduce them to his notice. He himself, after addressing them, commended them to their father's special care, and said, 'I intend to make something great of them.' "

Richelieu was a good promiser. Something great was made of them, but it was by no means he who did it.

In 1638, when Jacqueline was thirteen years old, a little collection of her poems was published, dedicated to the Queen, Anne of Austria. Several of the

pieces are addressed to this royal patroness ; some
are odes in honor of the Virgin and of St. Cecilia,
and there is quite an array of short epigrams and
love-songs, which seem strangely unnatural for a
child of that age, and utterly unlike herself as we
afterward know her. But that the little creature
took a serious view of her gift, and exercised it with
that conscientiousness which later became so strong
a characteristic, is evident from these

"Stanzas thanking God for the power of writing
Poetry."

> "Lord of the universe,
> If the strong chains of verse
> Round my delighted soul their links entwine,
> Here let me humbly own
> The gift is Thine alone,
> And comes, great God, from no desert of mine.
>
> "Yea, Lord, how many long
> For the sweet power of song,
> Which Thou hast placed in my young feeble heart ;
> Thy bounties string my lyre,
> And, with celestial fire,
> To my dull soul a hidden light impart.
>
> "O Lord, a thankless mind
> Will not acquittal find
> In Thy pure presence.  Therefore it is just
> That, touched with godlike flame,
> I should Thy love proclaim,
> And chant the glories of Thy Name august.
>
> "As waterfalls, and rills,
> And streams wind past the hills
> In steady progress toward their parent sea,

> Thus, Lord, my simple lays,
> Heedless of this world's praise,
> Find their way home, O Source Divine, to Thee!"

Dear little girl!  "Heedless of this world's praise!" That was the secret of her charm and the key-note of her character.  Many a child has been ruined by less flattering attentions than she received.  But she took all with a simple unconsciousness, that reminds one of the "little child set in the midst," from whom as a text the Great Teacher preached so grand a sermon.  She did not ignore her gift—"the sweet power of song"—perhaps even valued it more highly than it merited, but it did not fill her soul with vanity. It was not hers—it was a "gift."

"Though she wrote so much," says Gilberte, "and received so much attention, she did not lose in the least her gay good-humor.  She amused herself most heartily with her playmates in all childish games, and when alone, played with her dolls."

All this time Blaise was keeping up his studies, and distinguishing himself as much in science as Jacqueline in verse.

A girl as bright as she could not have been an uninterested looker-on at her brother's investigations and achievements.

We may safely conclude that the favorite little sister was not far away during his experiments on the nature of sound when he was about eleven years old. One day at table some one struck a china plate with a knife, producing, of course, a resonant vibration. But when a hand was placed on the plate the vibration suddenly ceased. " Why is this ? " asks the youthful philosopher, for " his earliest search," says his sister Gilberte, " is for *truth*. He must always have a reason that will satisfy his mind, and if none such is given him, he will not rest till he finds one for himself."

The answers of his elders, in the matter of the plate, did not satisfy him, and henceforth began a series of experiments on the laws of sound more systematic, if not less tuneful, than those of most boys of eleven, on the same subject. In the course of a few weeks he had noticed so many interesting facts that he wrote a treatise on the subject, which has been found by scientific men to be *tout à fait bien raissonné.*

A year later the boy was engaged in his famous geometrical investigations.

The story is, that seeing his strong bent toward mathematics, his father had purposely led his mind to other subjects, and, in fact, at last prohibited the study of geometry till after he had perfected himself in Latin and Greek. He gave him, however, in answer to repeated questions, the bare definition of the science as one that treated of " forms and their proportions and relations one to another."

On that hint Blaise went to work. In his hours of recreation he meditated on forms, and began to draw figures in charcoal on the walls of a large empty hall which had been given the children as a play-room. He made, at first, perfect circles, exact squares, and then a triangle whose sides and whose angles were equal, proving each step as he went along. All this was without a hint from any one, and he did not even know the names of the figures he drew. He called a circle "a round," and a line "a bar."

From his definitions sprang axioms, and from these demonstrations, and going from step to step, he had pushed his researches as far as the thirty-second proposition of the first book of Euclid before he was discovered. When his father found him proving that "the three angles of a triangle are together equal to two right angles," his question was, What had made him think of that? Oh, it followed from that other, said the boy; and the same question being asked in regard to that other, it was found that that followed from another earlier discovered truth. And, in this way, tracing his way back to first principles, his father saw how he had actually built up the science for himself out of a single definition.

As might be supposed, M. Pascal after this thought it right to remove the restriction on geometry, and gave his son a copy of Euclid's "Elements" for light reading. He insisted still, however, on the languages

as the principal and most serious work. But such
was the boy's delight in mathematics that he continued to prove and even to compose propositions for
his own amusement.

After a time his father occasionally took him to
the weekly meeting of scientific friends, out of which
association the celebrated "Academy of Sciences"
afterward grew. Descartes, Roberval, Pailleur, and
others whose names are familiar to the scientist were
members of this circle and *habitués* of M. Pascal's
house. At these meetings the boy Pascal is said to
have held his own in solving problems sent from
similar associations in Italy, Germany, Holland, and
other countries, and in offering original problems for
solution, and so clear and quick was his intellect that
he often discovered mistakes which no one else had
noticed. Sometimes he read short essays of his own,
and about the time Jacqueline's verses were published, he wrote in Latin a treatise on Conic Sec-
tions, which was considered very remarkable. Gilberte reports: "It was said that since the time of
Archimedes, nothing of such strength had appeared.
People skilled in such things said that it was a con-
tribution of permanent value to science, and thought
it should certainly be published. But my brother had
no desire for reputation. He took no interest in the
matter, and it was never printed."

# THE CARDINAL FROWNS ; THE CARDINAL SMILES.

# III.

## THE CARDINAL FROWNS; THE CARDINAL SMILES.

THE Pascals, one would say, were now at the very highest point of prosperity. They had wealth and position. They had the friendship of Royalty. They had the most congenial intimate friends, and a wide circle of distinguished acquaintance in the most brilliant city of the world. The son and heir was already giving extraordinary promise of remarkable and varied capacities—fairly on his way to the place Sir William Hamilton gives him as "a miracle of universal genius." The daughters seem endowed with loveliness and talent in equal parts. Surely M. Pascal ought to have been a proud and happy man!

This prosperity, moreover, was accompanied by that which alone makes other good things worth having. The glitter of the world seems never to have dazzled these wise people, even when they enjoyed it most. They saw about them many false and

hollow lives, many low ambitions, many weak, if
not evil characters. And these all were surrounded
by that bewildering halo—worldly success. But the
Pascals looked calmly on! They had before their
eyes a vastly higher ideal of life and of success.
They walked in the world, but, to a wonderful degree, they "kept unspotted." They were, in fact,
possessed of true nobility, and baseness, although
they touched it, could not cling to them.

Later, religious devotion became their most prominent characteristic. Now, great mental activity was
predominant. Yet, even at this time, a writer of the
day tells us that they were always regarded as "unusually religious people. In this respect they took
the lead of the society in which they moved." But
the Pascals were going on—still higher! and great
heights are not scaled without difficulty.

France just now was at war with Spain, and the
cardinal was in need of money. No easier way to
get it than to take it from the pockets of loyal Paris-
ians! And where this could not be done with a show
of legality it could be done, and was done, by arbi-
trary seizure of private property.

M. Pascal was one of many who suffered in this
way. His property, at this time, consisted largely of
shares in the *Hotel de Ville*, and his income, of
course, was much reduced when Richelieu seized
these bonds. He was not a man to take injustice

without an attempt at setting himself right. With others among the principal stockholders he remonstrated, appearing before the Chancellor of the city to make complaint, in March, 1638. The Chancellor, frightened, went to Richelieu, and Richelieu ordered the malcontents arrested and sent to the Bastile.

M. Pascal escaped this fate, but only by flight. He traveled *incognito* to his old home in Auvergne, and shortly after he left Paris the *halberdiers* came to look for him and were shown by Gilberte all over the house. "He had been much comforted," writes Gilberte, "under this affliction by Jacqueline's endearing ways. He loved her with unusual tenderness."

The father remained away through the whole summer, but in September he forgot all fear and hastened home again. His little daughter, Jacqueline, was seized with small-pox.

"Let the risk be what it might," says the family chronicler, "my father said he must then be at home in order to watch with his own eyes the course of her illness. And in reality he never left her for a moment, not even sleeping out of her room."

It was a long and serious case, and though the little girl recovered after many anxious weeks, "her countenance was quite disfigured, and she did not leave the house during the whole winter, not being fit to appear in company. She was then thirteen, old enough to value beauty, and to regret its loss. And yet, this mischance did not in the least trouble her; on the contrary, she considered it a mercy, and in some verses composed as a thank-offering for recovery, she said that her pitted face seemed to her the guardian of her innocence, and these traces of disease certain signs that God would keep her from evil. Though she was confined to the house, her time did not hang heavily, for she was busy with her trinkets and dolls."

The stanzas alluded to—"thanking God for recovery from the small-pox"—are rather sad for a little girl of thirteen, and not remarkably pretty. But their spirit is very sweet. These three verses will serve as a sample:

> " All men, great God, may see
>    Thy pure benignity
>        To one so weak and worn ;
>    Without Thy loving aid
>    Thus wondrously displayed,
> My life had faded in its April morn.

> " When, in the mirror, I
>    Scars of mine illness spy,
>        Those hollow marks attest
>    The heart-rejoicing truth,
>    That I am Thine, in sooth,
> For Thou dost chasten whom Thou lovest best.

> " I take them for a brand
>    That, Master, Thy kind hand
>        Would on my forehead leave,

> Mine innocence to show :—
> And shall I murmur? 'No.
> While Thy rod comforts me I will not grieve."

As soon as Jacqueline's recovery was secure, M. Pascal was obliged to exile himself once more. Whether the cardinal had been aware of his return, and with a little softening remembrance of the pretty children he had noticed in his audience-chamber, had winked at the fact, or whether the Pascals had succeeded in eluding his vigilance, we do not know. At any rate, they seem to have been entirely unmolested, and, in spite of Jacqueline's sad illness, to have passed many happy moments together.

But as soon as danger was over their father left them and spent the winter in Clermont. Some of the letters that passed between him and the children have been preserved, and toward spring there was truly something worth writing about.

The cardinal had taken a fancy to have a little play acted before him, and Jacqueline had been invited to take part in it!

From this it would seem that the little girl must have been getting better fast, and that she was not so seriously disfigured by her illness as was apprehended at first. Gilberte objects to her taking part in the play, not on the ground of health, but from a very natural unwillingness to favor Richelieu.

"The cardinal has not been so kind to us as to

2*

lead us to take any pains for his pleasure," she answered proudly, when the Duchess d'Aiguillon came to ask for Jacqueline's services.

The Duchess·d'Aiguillon was Richelieu's niece. She was a kind-hearted woman, and to her kindness she added a ready tact in humoring her uncle, which often enabled her to procure favors for those who had suffered by him. She knew, of course, all about the Pascals, and she saw a possible chance of M. Pascal's forgiveness and recall, if his little daughter should succeed in pleasing the cardinal.

On that ground she urged Gilberte to give her consent, and promised, meanwhile, to use every opportunity that presented itself of speaking a good word for her father. Gilberte still hesitated, but after asking the advice of some of her father's best friends she yielded, and Jacqueline forthwith began to study her part. It is mentioned, as a proof of the cardinal's false taste, that this play was not one of the masterpieces of French art, but a second-rate ephemeral tragi-comedy. What part Jacqueline took we do not know, but whatever it was, with so much at stake, she would be sure to enter into it with all her heart; moreover, she conceived the idea of playing a little private rôle of her own, and at once set her wits to work as to the best way of presenting that.

Her well-beloved talent for verse-making came to her aid, and she composed and committed to memory the following lines:

> "O marvel not, Armand*, the great, the wise,
>   If I have slightly pleased thine ear—thine eyes;
>   My sorrowing spirit torn by countless fears,
>   Each sound forbiddeth save the voice of tears;
>   With power to please thee, wouldst thou me inspire—
>   Recall from exile, now, my hapless sire."

The play came off on the evening of the third of April, 1639, in Richelieu's palace at Ruel.

"Jacqueline put into her action," says the Abbé Bossût, "a grace and a *finesse* which 'carried away' all the spectators, especially the cardinal himself, and she had the adroitness to profit by this moment of enthusiasm."

The rest of the story we will let Jacqueline herself tell in a letter she wrote her father the next day:

" M. le cardinal appeared to take great pleasure in the representation, especially when I spoke. He laughed very much and so did the whole company. When the play was finished, I came down from the stage to speak to Madame d'Aiguillon.

" But as the cardinal seemed about to leave, I went up to him at once, and recited to him the verses I send you. He received them with extraordinary affection and caresses, more than you can imagine. At first, when he saw me coming, he called out, 'Voilà la petite Pascal!' Then he embraced me and kissed me, and while I said my verses, he continued to hold me in his arms, and kissed me almost

---

*  Armand is Richelieu's family name.

every minute with great satisfaction. And then, when I was done, he said, 'Yes, I grant to you all that you ask; write to your father that he can return with safety.'

"Thereupon Madame d'Aiguillon approached, and spoke to the cardinal. 'Truly it would be well, sir, that you should do something for this gentleman. I have heard him spoken of as a thoroughly honorable and learned man, and it is a pity he should be useless to the government. Then he has a son who is very learned in mathematics, though only fifteen years old.'

"The cardinal again assured me that I might tell you to return in all safety; and as he seemed in such good humor, I asked him further, if you might come yourself to pay your thanks and respects to his eminence. He said you would be welcome; and afterwards, while talking of something else, he repeated, 'Tell your father when he returns, to come and see me.' This he said three or four times.

"After this, as Madame d'Aiguillon was going away, my sister went forward to take leave of her. She received her with many caresses, and inquired for our brother, whom she said she wished to know. So he was introduced to the duchess, and she paid him many compliments on his scientific attainments.

"We were then conducted to a room where we had a magnificent collation of dried sweetmeats, lemonade, fruits, and such things.

" Here the duchess renewed her caresses in a manner you will hardly believe. In short, I can not tell you how much honor I received, for I am obliged to write as briefly as possible. . . . . As for me, I feel myself extremely happy to have in any way assisted in a result which must give you satisfaction. It is what has always been the passionate wish of, M. my father, your very humble and obedient daughter and servant

" PASCAL."

After a long winter of convalescence in the house, more or less tedious even with trinkets and dolls to beguile the time, this evening of brilliant success, of " sweetmeats and lemonade," above all, of the accomplishment of her dearest hopes, must have been a wonderful thing to the little girl.

Gilberte tells the story a little differently, and accepting Cousin's opinion that " nothing should be neglected which will help us to become acquainted with this remarkable family," we give her version also :

"After the play Jacqueline came down to go with Madame de Saintot to the duchess, who was going to present her to the cardinal; but Madame de Saintot loitered, and seeing M. le cardinal rise as if to retire, Jacqueline ran up to him all alone. When he saw her coming he sat down again, took her on his knees, and when he kissed her again and again, she

began to weep. He asked her what was the matter.
Then she said her verse which Madame d'Aiguillon
followed with many obliging words; upon which M.
le cardinal said that he would grant the return of her
father. Then this little one, all of herself, without
any one knowing that she had thought of it, said:
'My lord, I have still one favor to ask of your eminence.' M. le cardinal was so captivated with the
delicacy of this little liberty that he answered: 'Ask
anything you wish, I will give it you.' She said to
him: 'I beg, your eminence, that my father may
have the honor of doing you reverence when he returns, and of thanking you for the favor you have
done us to-night.' The cardinal said: 'I not only
grant it, I wish it. Tell him to come with all assurance, and to bring his family with him.' "

Gilberte simply adds that on her father's return he
did go to thank the cardinal, and took them all with
him. But another account tells us that he went first
without his family, and when his name was announced Richelieu inquired if the gentleman was
alone. Hearing that he was, the servant was instructed to tell him that he could not have an audi-
ence till he came accompanied by his family. The
next day M. Pascal took all the children and was
most graciously received.

The cardinal after this treated him " handsomely,"
but he never gave him back his bonds.

# INTO NORMANDY.

INTO NORMANDY.

# IV.

### INTO NORMANDY.

YEAR of which we have no record now passed—a year, probably, of quiet happiness with our friends. There were the studies to be gone on with, and the good father was at home to be once more their teacher, and, though they were not so rich as they once had been, there were plenty of pleasures left.

But "in 1640," writes Gilberte, "my father, having been made colleague of M. de Paris, in the Intendancy of Normandy, was obliged to go to Rouen, and soon took us all there to live with him."

The office of Intendant was much like that of collector of customs with us. It was an honorable position, and a proof of Richelieu's continued friendliness. But in this case it was rather a difficult post, for Normandy was in a state of agitation and, in some parts, of open revolt. A new system of taxation had caused an insurrection of the peasantry in the neighborhood of Rouen, the rebels had defied the local authorities, destroyed the custom-house, and murdered some of the collectors.

M. Pascal and his colleague set out from Paris attended by a body of troops under Gassion, who is mentioned as a fierce man and a noted Calvinist.' On their entrance into Rouen they were met by an excited mob, through which they forced their way in the narrow winding streets, not without some bloodshed.

It was not an easy task to set to rights the public records and accounts, and the wide-awake Blaise conceived the idea of coming to his father's aid by the invention of a calculating machine. The notion was timely though the execution was not; for it was several years before he succeeded. The inventor's enthusiasm, however, never flagged, and in 1649, long after the necessity which had originally suggested it was past, the wonderful little instrument was patented. It was the parent of all the "adders" the world has since seen, and about as useful, practically, as the rest of them have proved. " The construction of such a machine," says a writer in the *North British Review*, " was a much more troublesome task than its contrivance, and Pascal not only injured his constitution, but wasted the most valuable portion of his life in his attempts to bring it to perfection."

The father's work, meanwhile, as we have said,

was done. And it was well done. M. Pascal's accuracy and, above all, his strict integrity in this difficult business is matter of comment on the part of more than one writer. He forbade his subordinates to accept the smallest gratuity, and discharged his secretary, a relative, for receiving a *louis d'or*.

As soon as Rouen was reduced to order, the family came to join their father, and here, in the same year, Gilberte was married to Florin Perier, a distant cousin of her father's. After her marriage she remained two years in Rouen, and then returned to the old home at Clermont. The other lived seven or eight years in Rouen; and for Jacqueline, opening womanhood here seems as full of brilliant promise as childhood in Paris.

Rouen was, and is, a most interesting city. Everybody stops there a few hours in making the journey between London and Paris. Everybody knows it as the most accessible clustering point of many fine specimens of rich mediæval Norman architecture. But when the city's five hundred bells pealed out on festival mornings in 1640, and Jacqueline Pascal threaded her way among churches and towers through the narrow streets to early Mass, a charm more sacred possessed her heart than that which can thrill the modern tourist at the same sound. The beautiful cathedral, with its glowing windows and springing arches, was to her not merely a sight to be seen,—

it was " none other than the house of God—the gate of heaven."

Sometimes Jacqueline must have crossed the old fish-market, and stopped, perhaps, for a moment beside the dripping fountain. The spot had already its history, though it was without its commemorative statue and its present inspiring name of " Place de la Pucelle." And there must have come to Jacqueline a nearer and more vivid thought than we can ever have, of the brave, pure girl who, two hundred years before, had there suffered at the stake because she would not swear to what she did not believe. Did a hint of what would one day be asked of herself ever cross Jacqueline's mind? And did a subtle inspiration of candor, enthusiasm, and courage come to her from the speaking stones of that dingy square? Undoubtedly;—for of such unsuspected influences are molded all our lives.

Rouen in 1640 was interesting not only from associations of the past. Its condition at that time was flourishing, its business good, its social advantages next, perhaps, to those of Paris. Corneille was living there, "and did not fail to visit us soon," says Gilberte.

To many modern readers, the name of Corneille is associated with school days—with dictionary and foot-notes blurring, rather than making clear, the beauties of his style. It is a little hard for such read-

ers to realize that he was a great poet—the Shake-
speare of France—the father of the French classical
drama. His greatest work, "The Cid," had been
published in 1638, and he was at the height of his
fame when the Pascals went to Rouen.

The rather peculiar, "hasty-tempered and blunt"
genius conceived a great liking for the poetess of
fifteen whose youthful fame had probably preceded
her. "He was ravished," says Gilberte, "with the
things which my sister wrote," and by his advice she
undertook a prize poem.— The city, according to
time-honored custom, awarded a prize every year to
the writer of the best poem on "The Conception of
the Virgin." Probably Corneille had received it so
often that he was thankful to find a possible successor. At any rate, he urged Jacqueline to compete,
and her effort, with others, was read to a great crowd
in the market-place, on the festival celebrating the
dogma in question. But "heedless," as in her childhood, "of this world's praise," when the President of
Ceremonies announced the awarding of the prize to
Mdlle. Jacqueline Pascal, the successful competitor
was not to be found, nor had she sent any representative to learn the decision. Her friend, Corneille,
however, rose and gave a graceful and flattering address of thanks in her name. The next day the prize
was brought to her house with drums, trumpets, and
a grand procession, "Yet," says Gilberte, "she re-

ceived it with remarkable indifference. She was so
very simple that, though she was then fifteen years
old, she always kept dolls, which she dressed and un-
dressed with as much pleasure as if she had been only
ten. We used to reproach her with this childishness,
and we did so so much that at last she was obliged to
give them up, though not without pain; for she
loved this diversion better than to take part in the
grandest fêtes in the city."

After Gilberte and her husband left Rouen, Jacqueline took up her position as head of the family,
and from that time till her twenty-first year led a life
of cheerful activity which is pleasant to think of.
Her brother's health now became delicate, bringing
out sisterly carefulness, not, as yet, exciting grave
anxiety. She studied with her father and brother,
and read more history and philosophy than most girls
of the seventeenth or of any century. And under
the advice of her friend Corneille, she continued to
write poetry. Some fugitive pieces of this period
were collected after her death by her niece, Margaret
Perier, and preserved among the annals of Port Royal,
and Cousin has given us a few others. But no published collection of her poems during her lifetime
followed the little volume of her thirteenth year.

We give two or three short specimens of verses
written at Rouen:

### SERENADE.

O pure and lovely Clarice, rise,
Bid sleep depart from those sweet eyes!

We blame thee not, that through the day
Thy charms should drive our peace away,
Then is it just for thee to sleep
While they who love thee vigil keep?

O mark the sorrows of my soul!
List to my sighs, and then console;
Or if thy heart I can not gain,
Lend me thine ear while I complain,
And since thy frowns forbid my sleep,
Share thou the weary watch I keep!

### DEVOTIONAL SONNET.

O glorious Architect of earth and sea,
   Yet of frail man the Maker and the stay,
   Here at Thine altar's foot I humbly pray,
Let Thy world-sheltering love encircle me.
Well may my every hope be built on Thee,
   For I can hear, unmoved, the thunder's growl,
   Can brave e'en demons and their whispers foul
When my heart trusteth in Thy sure decree.

But, ah! the power of sin o'erwhelms my frame,
Frustrates my wishes, makes my spirit tame,
And dims the lustre of its zealous flame.
Its languor pardon, Lord! my strength uphold,
Make my weak nature in Thy service bold,
Let not Thy love in my faint heart wax cold!

The following is interesting, as showing that some
of Jacqueline's associates must have been Protestants.

Poor girl! It is touching to see how she struggles
between a natural affection for a lovely character and
a horror of heretical doctrine:

ON THE DEATH OF A HUGUENOT LADY.

Friendly tears were never shed
O'er a lovelier lady dead :
Chloris was, in form and face,
Gifted with angelic grace ;
But in youth's enchanting bloom,
Fate has laid her in the tomb.

We have deeper cause to groan
O'er her state a shade is thrown ;
Anxious doubts our spirits chafe
As we ask, " Can she be safe ?—
She who died, remaining still
A heretic in act and will ?"

Doubt not, in the dying hour,
That her strengthened soul had power,
By afflictions purified,
Every weight to cast aside,—
Light celestial entering in,
That she meekly owned her sin.

And, O Lord, if earthly love
Can Thy tender pity move,
Hear the prayers we'll henceforth make
In Thy temple for her sake
Whom Thou didst create so fair,
But who never worshiped there.

Her ill-fated birth alone
Caused the errors we bemoan ;
Blinded by her zeal's excess,
And her filial tenderness,

To the last she persevered
In the faith her sire revered.

Thou didst on her spirit shower
Heavenly gifts, the precious dower
Of the souls that love Thee best;—
Calm devotion filled her breast,
And the flame of sacred love
Raised her hopes to Thee above.

Day by day her dearest care
Was to serve her Lord by prayer.
Could her faith so fruitful be
If it were not given of Thee?
Shall the zeal Thou didst bestow
Sink her in eternal woe?

In my dim and sinful state,
Lord, I dare not penetrate
Secrets that Thy wisdom hides,
But Thy goodness yet abides;—
And Thine equitable will
Is with mercy tempered still.

Doubtless Jacqueline already took a lively interest
in the great religious questions which then agitated
France and, indeed, all Europe. She could not have
failed often to hear them discussed. At that time,
and for about twenty years afterward, the Huguenots
were tolerated, and many of the noblest families of
the land openly avowed the reformed faith. Yet
though treated with an outward show of respect they
were never cordially regarded or fairly dealt with by
either Church or Court. At the bottom of all politi-

3

cal turbulence boiled always these fierce religious disputes, and now and then all other issues would be forgotten and overwhelmed in their fury. Catholic and Huguenot armies had, for a century, in turn devastated the land. And even when times were most peaceful the great questions, in one shape or other, were working in men's minds. With Luther on one side and Calvin on the other, France could not escape these questions. Even the Church could not remain uninfluenced, and consciously or unconsciously, in small or in great degree, and with a thousand varying shades of understanding, faithful Catholics were weighing the new thoughts, looking at truth in the new ways. Little did Jacqueline Pascal guess how near her the leaven was working!

Cousin, referring to these years in Rouen, says of our heroine: " Her personal attractions, her charming character, her modesty, her sprightliness, her talents, her reputation, made her the ornament of all the most elegant and distinguished society. She lived there till the middle of 1646, that is to say, till she was twenty years old, pious and regular, but without any exaggeration of these traits, far from the thought of becoming a nun, more than once sought in marriage, increasing in grace and in talent under the fostering wings of an incomparable family, among the friends of her father and her brother, and under the immediate guidance of the great Corneille, who was then in all the force of his genius and in the full brilliancy of his glory."

Gilberte affectionately reviews the same period in these words:

"The reputation which she had acquired by the '*gentillesses*' of her childhood did not diminish as she grew older; on the contrary, it went on always augmenting. She had the great qualities of every period of life. She was popular with all sorts of people, and those who were not intimate with her sought her acquaintance most eagerly. When she appeared in any company, you could see how every one rejoiced at her coming, and a little murmur of pleasure would rise; *and she always satisfied those who expected something pleasant of her.*"

# A FLEMISH BISHOP.

# V.

## A FLEMISH BISHOP.

AND now let us turn away from Rouen for a time and look across low-lying fields and slow, broad streams, into a quiet bishop's study in Flanders. A little backward in time our glance must go, for, in 1638, that spring after Jacqueline Pascal had played her part so well before Richelieu, this bishop, Cornelius Jansen, died. Probably she had never heard of him at that time; but two years afterward all Europe began to ring with his name, for his great book, the work of his life—the "Augustinus"—was then published. Twenty years the patient scholar had labored on this work, till the very life and essence of his being seemed absorbed into it, and the day he wrote the final page was the day of his death.

Jansen was born in 1585, and educated for the priesthood at the Jesuit college of Louvain. There, when nineteen years old, he stood "first scholar of the university," and always and everywhere scholarship was his most prominent characteristic. He was one of those men who never look like themselves unless they have a book under their arm. His "dear delight" was patient investigation, comparison, criticism. His mind was not eager and grasping like Blaise Pascal's, but careful, searching, microscopic.

In youth Jansen formed a lifelong friendship with a young Frenchman from Bayonne—Jean du Verger de Hauranne, afterward Abbé de St. Cyran, and known in history by that name.

At Paris the friends studied theology together, and, to their surprise, they found theology to mean, not the science of God, but the writings of the schoolmen, endless and fruitless disputations, subtle casuistries, all sorts of intellectual puzzles and paradoxes. Both of the young men were fond of such mental gymnastics, and we have specimens of disquisitions written by each at about this time which seem to any straightforward, clear-thinking person the sheerest waste of the reasoning powers. But the minds of Jansen and St. Cyran were not only acute; they were earnest, sincere, devout. They soon saw that all this tilting and tourneying was but a sorry mockery of true Christian warfare. They longed for something that went deeper; and Jansen, walking in his garden, was often observed to lift his eyes to heaven and murmur, "Oh, truth! truth!"

The friends made up their minds that pure doctrine

could only be obtained by going back to the Fathers of the Church. And they went back—as far as St. Augustine! If only it had occurred to them to go a little farther! If only they had reached the purer streams fed more directly from the Fountain! If only they had pushed their way to the "well of water" itself, and there drunk of the Truth for which they thirsted!

However, they went back to St. Augustine, and after leaving Paris, Jansen made a six years' visit to his friend at Bayonne, where they pursued together the study of their chosen author. Jansen's health was most delicate and precarious, but he would pay no attention to his poor body. He studied almost without ceasing, seldom going to bed, his biographers tell us, but passing day and night in a large chair, fitted up with cushions and writing-desk. Here, when fatigue overcame him, he would rest and sleep for a time. His maximum of sleep was four hours out of the twenty-four.

"My son," complained St. Cyran's careful mother, "you will certainly kill your good Fleming if you let him work so hard." But neither St. Cyran nor his mother could help it.

The student's only answer to remonstrance was that he wished he had lived in the time of Joshua, when "the sun stood still in the midst of heaven," or that he could "follow the cranes in their northward flight and find places where the day should be nineteen or twenty hours long."

It is a comfort to know that, between the chapters of St. Augustine, he allowed himself a game of battledore and shuttlecock with St. Cyran, and that they attained great proficiency, sometimes scoring three or four thousand.

At the end of six years the friends separated. Jansen went home to Flanders to take a professorship at Louvain, and afterward the bishopric of Ypres. At the same time he worked constantly on his beloved "Augustinus." Ten times, we are told, he carefully read through the whole body of St. Augustine's works. Thirty times he read certain parts, sifting, comparing, nicely weighing every word. Besides all this, he thoroughly studied every passage throughout the voluminous works of the other Fathers which bore in the least on the doctrines of St. Augustine. Truly, as the annalist of Port Royal temperately remarks, "when we consider that Jansenius digested and arranged in twenty years the whole mass of sacred literature accumulated in thirteen centuries, it excites astonishment!"

At last, at the end of the twenty years, the scholar's meagre face begins to shine. For some days his servants notice that his countenance is illumined as with a great joy. He is putting the finishing touches to the work of his life. He is crowning the idol of his heart. "The burning joy consumes him," says Sainte-Beuve. He writes the final word. He is seized with the plague and dies in less than twenty-four hours.*

His will, written half an hour before his death, thus disposes of his sole treasure, his precious book: "I now lay my work at the feet of his Holiness. I submit its contents to his decision, approving, condemning, advancing, or retracting whatever shall be prescribed by the thunders of the Apostolic See." And so Cornelius Jansen left his work to follow him, and went on, we feel sure, to study more glorious truth than his heart had yet conceived.

The world will always, and very justly, look at Jansen chiefly as a scholar. But he somewhat touchingly deprecates being thought "a mere pedant of the schools," and it is pleasant to see, by occasional flashes, that he is something more. Like many another silent, bookish man, he could show upon occasion great personal bravery. In his many disputes with the Jesuits he displayed an address and sagacity that surprised his best friends. What is more, he usually gained his point—a fact which the Jesuits never forgot and never forgave.

---

* One account eulogizes Jansen's courage and devotion to the poor during the prevalence of the plague just before he died. But Sainte-Beuve declares his to have been an isolated instance of the disease, and suggests that it may have been communicated by some of the old manuscripts over which he pored.

As bishop he was kind and accessible, always dropping his pen with a beautiful alacrity at the call of the poor or distressed.

His intimacy with St. Cyran reveals beneath the scholar's quiet breast another unsuspected thing—a well of simple tenderness, pure and deep. After the long stay together at Bayonne, Jansen writes to his friend that when the first letter came he was not alone, and was forced to imitate the patriarch Joseph and "go out and seek where to weep." After another visit, he alludes to the tears each shed at parting; and again, speaking of an expected meeting, he joyfully says that he is traveling toward his friend, and has arranged to "enter France with the month of May."

An earnestness was given to this friendship by their common choice of Abraham as their model character. During their studies at Paris, they had been struck by the sublimity of Abraham's faith. They felt humbled before the man who, without the Church, without the saints and Mary, without the full knowledge of the Lord Jesus Christ, without even the Mosaic law, had so nearly attained obedience to the divine command, "Walk before me, and be thou *perfect.*"

This command they resolved to take for their own, and thus

> "Aiming at a star,
> Shot higher far than he that means a tree."

And now about this great book of Cornelius Jansen's—this "Augustinus." How many of us have ever seen it, or, indeed, heard of it before? Sainte-Beuve says of it, that "no book of its calibre ever became so famous, while remaining so little known." Another writer speaks of it as "celebrated almost alone for the evils it occasioned." The great majority of those who bore the name of Jansenist—gladly bore it to prison and to death—never read the ponderous tomes. Fewer still ever saw the man who wrote them.

The "Augustinus" was written in Latin, and was, in short, a "tissue of texts from St. Augustine." These were arranged with consummate nicety and skill, so as to bring out the complete system of the Augustinian doctrines.

It is not for this little book of ours to unfold these doctrines. Enough for us to know that they are, in effect, the system known to us as Calvinism. Enough for us to see, as we shall see in going on with this story, that the Jansenists, whatever their beliefs, were "a fountain of sweet waters in the midst of the brackish sea"—a "learned and religious society in the bosom of the Catholic Church, who distinctly taught justification by faith, and were assiduously occupied in the dissemination of the Scriptures." Just a step more, and a very short step, too, and every one of them would have become that accursed thing, a Huguenot!

Indeed, as we shall see, they did come near enough this point to take their share of persecution. The Jesuits, with artifice all their own, distorted and rendered ambiguous certain parts of the "Augustinus," and then secured their condemnation by the pope. They dishonored and destroyed the author's tomb. They tortured and imprisoned his friends.

Jansen's was, indeed, a singular destiny! To give his name to, and be condemned for, a system of doctrines not his own, but that of a recognized, canonized saint, and to be the exciting cause of bitter strife in which he took no part! His own life, as we have seen, flowed still as the streams of his native land, and when the billows rose he was safe beyond their power in his eternal Home.

# THE DIRECTOR OF CONSCIENCES.

# VI.

## THE DIRECTOR OF CONSCIENCES.

S T. CYRAN was a very different man from Jansen. He was charged to the full with that personal magnetism which his friend utterly lacked. He was a man of commanding presence, "tall and majestic in form," his biographers tell us, and of a very noble countenance.

His "firm, penetrating eye," his gentleness and courtesy, and a certain elevation in his manners, combined to render him almost irresistible. His friends and followers were full of admiring enthusiasm for him, and, as they admired, he "silently, but certainly" governed them.

When Jansen went back to Flanders after their six years' visit together at Bayonne, St. Cyran went to Poitiers, where he was appointed canon of the cathedral. He passed rapidly from one honorable position to another, the last being the abbacy of the monastery which gives him his name. But in five years from the time he left Bayonne, we find him in Paris living the life of a simple priest. He was a man of wealth and could live as he chose, and he chose retirement and simplicity. But greatness pursued him and would not let him go. He soon acquired reputation and influence as a confessor, or, as he much preferred to be called, "a director of consciences."

Cardinal Richelieu had known St. Cyran in his youth, and he was keen enough to recognize now all the man's power. At the same time he did not love him any too well. For one thing, they did not agree on doctrinal points. Did not St. Cyran teach that love of God was essential to true faith, while Richelieu held that fear of punishment was all that was needed? And was he not known to have declared that absolution and remission of sins belong to God alone?

Moreover, it is said that St. Cyran knew some disreputable secrets in regard to the cardinal's life, which that prelate might well prefer not to have remembered by such a man. Under these circumstances, Richelieu did just what we should have expected him to do. He tried St. Cyran first with craftiness, then with cruelty.

St. Cyran was promptly introduced by the cardinal at court, as "the most learned man in Europe." This was a polite fiction, as both parties knew. It would have been much nearer the truth if spoken of Jansen.

Next, Richelieu offered him the position of first almoner to Henrietta of England, the French princess who had married Charles the First. This was a most politic move. The office was honorable enough to satisfy almost any man's ambition, and, at the same time, it would remove St. Cyran—secrets and all—from the society where he was beginning to have such remarkable influence. But St. Cyran calmly declined the honor and thus avoided the snare.

Eight bishoprics were then successively offered him, among them the very desirable ones of Clermont and Bayonne. After each of these offers, St. Cyran attended the cardinal's levée, and courteously thanked him for his kind intentions. But he never attended courtly festivities on other occasions, and withdrew himself more and more from the fashionable society which had been so ready to welcome him.

He took an humble lodging opposite the Carthusian convent and devoted himself to prayer, study, and charity. But it was like the leaven hidden in the meal. Obscurity only seemed to widen his influence. He was not seen among the guests of the wealthy, but here, in this modest retreat, he daily received visits from those who were wont to be found in the audience-chambers of the Palais Royal and the Louvre.

He was a physician of souls, and many a pained and weary heart, half unconscious, perhaps, of its own ailment, and ignorant of the remedy, came here to him for help. With wonderful patience, tenderness, and skill, though sometimes with a keen and painful probing, he laid bare the hidden disease and showed the way to the Healer.

It was not only by the wealthy and fashionable that he was sought. The greatest thinkers of his time, lawyers, statesmen, scientists, priests, came to be directed by him, and, one by one, he led them away from their errors into the truth.

Devout and thoughtful women who had been praying for years under the silent convent roof, and whose hearts God had been slowly opening, now heard of this new teacher, sent, as it seemed to them, from God, and came to put themselves under his guidance.

Angélique and Agnes Arnauld, the celebrated sister abbesses of Port Royal (with whom through our friends, the Pascals, we are soon to become familiar), early sought for themselves and their nuns St. Cyran's influence, and he became the regular spiritual director of their convent.

Long ago, in their own Bibles and through their own enlightened consciences, partly, perhaps, though they never guessed it, through the influence of Huguenot relatives, these sisters had found out for

themselves something of this more excellent way.
Now, how good it was to be confirmed and strengthened by this holy man! How wisely he instructed
all these nuns, and helped them make of the dull
routine of the convent a happy service for the Master's sake! How he smoothed away intellectual
doubts and difficulties for the more thoughtful ones!
How he helped and advised them in every way, and
how warmly and womanly they all loved him!

But he was very sharp with them sometimes, so
much so that Angélique (who, as we shall see, had
some spirit of her own) one day said to him, "My
father, it seems to me you are only gentle toward
those who abuse your confidence and deceive you."

When Marie-Claire, another of the Arnauld sisters,
who had been very unjust to St. Cyran in a certain
matter, came, at last, almost broken-hearted in her
penitence, to make her humble confession, he stopped her.

"We must find out," he said, "whether you exag-
gerate your faults, and whether in the sight of God they
are as great as you think them. We must look carefully into this matter. . . . . God is a Spirit, and
spiritual sins grieve Him more than any others.
Beware of exaggeration. We do not need any close
scrutiny to remind us of our sins. Kneel before God
without words, without anxious self-scrutiny. He
will understand you."

Another day when she was mourning over her sins, he said : "You must forget the past. If we were always obliged to think of our past sins, no one could be happy. He who has commanded us not to look back when we have put our hand to the plow, knows what is for our good."

When Marie-Claire begged that she might as a penance, and in proof of her humility, be made a lay sister* for life, St Cyran sharply rebuked her.

"You wish the future to be settled for you," he said. "I do not like that request. Those who belong to God ought to have nothing absolutely settled and decided. . . . . For myself, I do not want to know what I shall do when I leave this place. We are told to ask God for our bread (that is, for His grace), day by day; but I should like to ask for it hour by hour. . . . . It is contrary to the spirit of true humility to seek to do extraordinary things. There is no greater pride than in seeking to humiliate ourselves beyond measure ; and sometimes there is no truer humility than to attempt great works for God."

Many a word of wisdom taken direct from the good man's lips, and many a delightful anecdote of him or his distinguished friends, is recorded for us in Lancelot's charming "Mémoires de St. Cyran." The

---

* A lay-sister is one who performs the menial services of the convent.

pen is tempted to linger over them, but we must content ourselves with a very few.

Notwithstanding his ordinarily cool and dignified demeanor, the good father had a very tender spot in his heart, especially toward the little ones. One day he bought a pot of preserved quinces for a little girl among the novices at Port Royal, a daughter of his particular friend, d'Andilly. But on the way to the convent, scruples overcame him lest "the sweets of earth should destroy her taste for the sweets of heaven." He resolved not to offer the gift, and hid it under the folds of his mantle. But when he reached the house and was told that the little girl was not feeling well that day, love overcame his caution, and the quinces were sent to her room at once.

A conscientious nun once came to him very much exercised in regard to the faults of a certain sister nun. Surely these were very wrong proceedings. Should she speak of them? "Be silent for three months," said the director of consciences. At the end of three months she reminded him that the time had elapsed. Might she tell now? "No," said he, "be silent for the rest of your life."

De Séricourt, who had been a military man, after his conversion asked St. Cyran to teach him how to pray. "You know soldiers are not much instructed on this point," he said.

St. Cyran placed his hands together, bowed his head, and then lifted his eyes to heaven. "This, sir, is all we have to do," he said. "We have only to appear humbly before God, and remember that He is looking down upon us." De Séricourt says that his master's devout look and these simple words were better than all the books of devotion in the world.

To his learned body of "Recluses," all of them, in spite of their religious ardor, more or less ambitious of literary fame, St. Cyran one day said: "Jesus Christ has written nothing; and He shows us thereby that the sublimity of godliness can only be worthily represented by *living acts.*"

As may easily be seen, a man teaching such pure and undefiled religion as this, and exercising such a powerful and wide-spread influence, was an element not very desirable to a corrupt Church.

The Jesuits hated him as heartily as Richelieu did, and that not merely on doctrinal grounds, but also from a very natural feeling of jealousy and envy.

Up to this time the schools of the Jesuits had enjoyed great celebrity. The education of the higher classes had been almost entirely in their hands. But now, among St. Cyran's friends there were many persons of rank and fortune who wished equal advantages for their children without the contamination of Jesuitical principles.

They consulted St. Cyran, and, under his personal

direction, a number of little schools in and about Paris were opened.

There were plenty of men of talent among his disciples to take the place of teachers. Nicole, Lancelot, and Fontaine, all of whom have written long and intensely interesting histories of these times, were among them. "The great Arnauld," foremost of a remarkable family, was a writer of text-books for these schools, and so was De Saci, the author of that beautiful, "pure, limpid translation of the Bible" still in use among French Protestant churches.

A few years later we shall find Blaise Pascal adding to the fame of these schools by his novel and successful theories of education, and Racine, the poet, entering one of them as a pupil.

The "Port Royal Grammars" (Greek and Latin), the "Greek Primitives," and the "Elements of Logic and of Geometry," were soon famous, not only throughout France, but throughout Europe.

Learned treatises on many subjects, but chiefly on theology, were published by those connected with these schools, and *"Ils sont marqués au coin de Port Royal"** came to be the fashionable phrase of condemnation, or favor, as the case might be.

* From the fact that a large number of St. Cyran's followers who called themselves "the recluses," but were bound by no vows, established themselves at the gates of the convent of Port Royal

Clearly, as we have said, this state of things was no longer to be borne, and we are not surprised to learn that after seventeen years in Paris, St. Cyran was one day arrested by order of the cardinal. Nineteen separate charges Richelieu averred that he found against this seditious priest, but the charges were never specified, for there was no trial, and, until he had been a year in prison, no show even of examination. At midnight, May 14, 1638, twenty-two archers surrounded St. Cyran's little dwelling and waited until morning, hoping to find some pretext for attacking the house; but nothing of the kind occurring, at six o'clock they knocked and demanded admission. St. Cyran was reading St. Augustine with his nephew, and they had just come to a passage on humility. "That is just what we want," he said. "Here is something to defend ourselves with." The officer then coming into his room informed him that he had orders to conduct him to a carriage standing at the gate. "Sir," said St. Cyran, kindly taking his hand, "it is my duty and my pleasure to obey the King."

They drove at once to the fortress of Vincennes. Many a traveler of our day has taken the same road through the grand old park and forest to the chateau, and climbed the ruined *donjon* for the magnificent

_______________

des Champs, eighteen miles from Paris, the whole party were often called Port Royalists, though after the death of Jansen, from their defense of his book, they were frequently called Jansenists.

view of the surrounding country and the distant city. As they went through the park they met M. d'Andilly, that friend whom St. Cyran called his "friend *par excellence.*" Lancelot tells us that the guard had received orders to turn back the facings of their regimentals so as to excite no suspicion. Consequently d'Andilly, with no thought of trouble, rode gaily up to the side of the coach and said: "My father, where are you taking all these people?" "It is not I who take them; they take me," answered St. Cyran. "But," he added, "I look upon myself as the prisoner of God, not of man."

The friends were allowed a few moments' conversation, when St. Cyran mentioned his regret that he could not have had time to bring a book with him. D'Andilly had with him a copy of the confessions of St. Augustine. "You first taught me the value of this book," he said. "Now I am thankful to give it back to you." "They then embraced," says the touching story, "as those who expect to see each other's face no more till the resurrection of the just."

The same morning Richelieu called to him one of his attendant ecclesiastics. "Beaumont," said he, "I have done a thing which will raise a great outcry. I have had the Abbot of St. Cyran arrested. Learned people and pious people, too, will make a great piece of work about it. But I am sure I have done a good thing. A great many calamities would have been averted if Luther and Calvin had been shut up as soon as they began to dogmatize."

And some time later, when Prince Henry of Bourbon ventured to plead for St. Cyran, the cardinal answered, "You don't know the man for whom you are interceding.   He is more dangerous than six armies.'

# "THE OBSTACLE BECOMES THE INSTRUMENT."

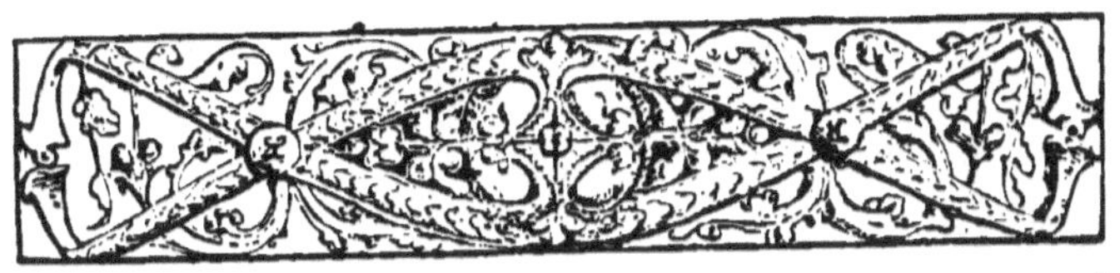

# VII.

## " THE OBSTACLE BECOMES THE INSTRUMENT."

IN the prison of Vincennes, at the time of St. Cyran's arrest, was a certain learned priest named Guillebert. He was released soon afterward, but not till he had heartily adopted St. Cyran's views and begun to seek the truth in his spirit.

When he was set free he was appointed to the parish of Rouville, a suburb of Rouen. And thus we come around—the circle of circumstance and influence being complete—to the Pascals once more.

For as soon as Guillebert began to preach he became famous in all the region round about. "A great religious awakening "—the phrase has an oddly constrained and "not at home " look in the French—took place throughout the whole diocese of Rouen.

Father Guillebert was eloquent as well as learned, and this fact, added to the novelty and force of his teachings, brought all sorts of people, from far and from near, to hear him. Rouville was crowded with guests, and members of the parliament of Rouen were accustomed to hire lodgings in the village of a Saturday so as to be ready for the Sabbath services. Sunday traveling was, apparently, not so fashionable then as it has since become.

The new doctrines became the town talk of Rouen, and, whatever their opinion concerning them, the Pascals must have shared in the general interest, and very possibly were sometimes among Guillebert's hearers. But, for a year or two after Madame Perier's marriage, we lose her graphic family narrative, and have no record of the details of their life.

Sainte-Beuve thinks he can trace in Corneille's writings after this time the influence of the truths preached at Rouville, though the poet, educated by the Jesuits, and closely connected with them in many ways, remained through life attached to that party. However this may be, no intelligent person living at this time in Rouen could have failed to be more or less affected by these things, and the Pascals had doubtless before this watched with interest the cardinal's proceedings against St. Cyran.

It was at last, however, by one of those seeming accidents on which so often human destinies are hinged, that these solemn questions of truth and duty became vital realities to our friends. Up to this time they had been upright, conscientious, devout, but not, as they expressed it, " éclairé."

One day, in the winter of 1646, M. Pascal slipped and fell on the ice, seriously spraining or dislocating his thigh. One account mentions that it was "while absent from home on a charitable errand" that the accident took place.

Now there were living in the neighborhood of Rouen two wealthy gentlemen, brothers, named Deslandes and De la Bouteillerie,* who seem to have been surgeons by nature, and who were often called upon to remedy such accidents.

These gentlemen had become, under the preaching of Guillebert, humble and active Christians. Each of them had erected a small hospital in his own park, Deslandes, who had ten children, furnishing his building with ten beds and De la Bouteillerie, who was childless, providing for twice that number of patients. Both spent most of their time in attendance on the sick, and they were always ready at any call to exercise their remarkable skill in setting broken or dislocated bones.

M. Pascal "placed no confidence in any one else," his daughter tells us, and sent at once for these good brothers, who not only came, but, both of them, remained in the family three months in order to insure complete recovery.

This was the turning point in Jacqueline Pascal's

---

* Brothers in French families are often known by different names according to their estates.

4*

life. These three months were the quick, warm summer sent to ripen the character we have seen already in its fragrant flower. True, conscientious, enthusiastic—much that was right and lovely and pure—she had been before. She now becomes (and recognizes herself as such) a loving child of God. She now seeks first His kingdom and His righteousness, and all these other things are added unto her.

Just when the change came we can not know.

> " Who ever saw the earliest rose
> First open her sweet breast ?
> Or, when the summer sun goes down,
> The first soft star in evening's crown
> Light up her gleaming crest ? "

But at some time during this period the influences of all her past life, gracious and merciful, and leading always up to this point, culminated in the influences of the moment, and she stepped into a larger life— she became partaker of the Eternal Life.

"Toward the end of the year 1646, about ten months after the accident," writes Gilberte, "when M. Bellay, the bishop of the diocese, was holding an ordination at Rouen, my sister, who had not yet been confirmed, wished to receive this sacrament. She prepared for it according to instructions which she found in some little treatises of M. de St. Cyran, and we have reason to believe that she then truly received the Holy Spirit, for, from that time, she was greatly changed."

The residence of these two physicians with the Pascals did not affect Jacqueline alone. The whole household profited by their presence. Their improving conversation and the simple goodness of their lives, we are told, first attracted the hearts of all, and then there came the natural curiosity to see the books which they mentioned as having been helpful and inspiring to them.

"Thus they became acquainted," says Madame Perier, "with the works of M. Jansen, M. de St. Cyran, M. Arnauld, and with other writings by which they were greatly edified."

Blaise, with his eager, searching mind, was not long in investigating the truths now brought so near to him. And, once carefully considered, he honestly and heartily adopted them, and gave up his life to the service of God. "He comprehended perfectly," says his sister, "that the Christian religion obliges us to live for God alone, and to have no other object, and this truth appeared to him so evident, so necessary, and so practical, that he brought to an end all his researches, and from that time renounced all other knowledge to apply himself alone to that 'one thing' which Jesus Christ calls needful."

In "giving up all other knowledge and terminating all his researches," Blaise Pascal went through, as we

shall see, a terrible struggle—it may seem to us a
needlessly violent one. But one temptation he did
not have. Skepticism, which has troubled so many
minds before his day and since, seems never to have
attacked him. He had no doubts in regard to the
vital and eternal truths of Christianity. His grasp of
mind was so large and his intellect so clear that he
did not confuse, as so many have done, the different
realms of truth. He recognized that spiritual things
can not be discerned as material things are discerned,
or judged as material things are judged. His wise
father had "taught him from infancy that that
which is the object of faith can not be the object
of reason, much less can it be submitted to reason."
"This maxim, often reiterated by a father for whom
he had great respect, and in whom he saw great
knowledge, accompanied with a very clear and
powerful reason, made so great an impression on his
mind that, whatever discourse he may have heard
which tended to free-thinking, he was in no way
moved by it; and even when he was very young, he
regarded skeptics as men who were acting on a false
principle, viz, that the human reason is above everything else, and as men who did not understand the
nature of faith."

"Thus," continues Madame Perier, "this mind, so
large, so grasping, and so full of curiosity, which
searched with so much care for the cause and the

reason of everything, was, at the same time, in matters of religion, trustful as a little child.

"This simplicity governed his whole life, so that, in after-years, when his whole heart was engrossed with spiritual realities, he never busied himself with curious questions of theology, but applied the full strength of his mind to understand and to practice Christian holiness, dedicating to this all his talents, and meditating day and night on the law of his God."

What a Christian character was that! Happy Jacqueline, who could walk hand in hand with such a brother in the way which, though they found it narrow, they also found a way of exceeding pleasantness! Happy father, who now, "not ashamed to become the child of his children," followed after them in this way of life!

In the course of the winter M. and Madame Perier visited Rouen and became the subjects of a like change. And thus the whole family rejoiced together in the love of God, and entered with enthusiastic devotion on the highest service possible to human souls.

During the years immediately preceding the conversion of the Pascals, great changes had taken place in France.

In December, 1642, Cardinal Richelieu died, and a few months afterward, the king, Louis XIII., leaving the kingdom in the hands of Anne of Austria as Regent, with Cardinal Mazarin for Prime Minister.

The young king, Louis XIV., was but five years of age at the time of his father's death.

When Richelieu died, many a prison-door was opened, and among those liberated was St. Cyran. His years in prison had been fruitful ones. As is so often the case in the lives of good men, "the obstacle became the instrument," and the letters written from his cell and circulated with enthusiastic industry by his friends and disciples, probably did more good than he, in his own person, could have effected. Especially was religious interest quickened among the nobility by Richelieu's violent measure.

The Duchess d'Aiguillon interceded with her uncle for St. Cyran, but without the success which had attended her efforts for M. Pascal during Jacqueline's childhood. She obtained permission, however, to visit the prisoner and to take d'Andilly with her, and through this latter faithful friend St. Cyran was kept supplied with pencils and paper. The duchess also visited Port Royal, and the convent became, we are told, "a fashionable resort of the court," much to the discomfort of the good abbesses Angélique and Agnes. They were willing, however, to do what they could for human souls, whatever their station in this life. They showed infinite patience, tenderness, and charity toward the Princess de Guemené, for example, who was one of their most constant visitors, but a woman of light and frivolous character. Her frequent " retreats " to the convent, and her long conversations with them on spiritual matters gave them great hope of her. But St. Cyran, to whom all these things were faithfully reported, knew the world better than they did. " The grace of God in that woman's soul," he wrote, "is like a spark kindled on an icy pavement with the winds blowing on it from every quarter." And so it proved.

But in some seemingly unpromising spots the well-tended spark increased to a flame both warm and bright. Among the " illustrious women of the seventeenth century " (of whom Cousin has given us some delightful studies, and first of whom, by the way, he places our own Jacqueline Pascal), we find many whose hearts have caught, in greater or less degree, the gracious warmth and light.

A beautiful example of thorough and sincere conversion was Madame de St. Ange, a member of the household of Anne of Austria. This lady, we are told, " was soon promoted by St. Cyran from the rank of disciple to that of friend," and she became one of the most faithful of his agents in the distribution of charity.

Pleasant stories are told of St. Cyran's thoughtful kindness for others while in prison. At one time he bestows a wedding dowry on a poor maiden. Again, he sends for a black coat for a poor mad prisoner who can not endure the sight of the gray clothes he wears.

Among the prisoners were a Baron and Baroness de Beausoleil, who were very destitute and poorly clad. St. Cyran sent directions to have clothing bought for them, and added: " Pray let the cloth be good and fine, such as befits their rank. I do not know what is proper, but I think I have heard somewhere that gentlemen and ladies of their condition can not appear without gold lace for the men and black lace for the women. If so, pray get the best, and, in short, let all be done modestly, but yet handsomely, that, in looking at each other, they may for a few minutes forget that they are captives."

Against this waste his almoner remonstrated. ("Why was not this ointment sold for three hundred pence and given to the poor?") But St. Cyran answered: "I do not believe that the Lord, who commands me to give unto Cæsar that which is Cæsar's, will account me a bad steward for giving modestly to each according to that rank in which *He* placed them." Let us ponder this lesson—all of us active philanthropists who are so much inclined to give to the needy not what they wish, but what we think they ought to wish—who willingly "bestow our goods to feed the poor, and have not charity."

As we have seen in the case of Guillebert, St. Cyran's influence on his fellow-prisoners often produced wide-spread results. All were, at least, impressed by his character, if not convinced by his teachings.

John de Wert, a Spanish nobleman and prisoner of war, who was also at Vincennes, was once released for a few days on parole, and invited to a magnificent *ballet* given by Richelieu for the express purpose of impressing the foreign ministers and prisoners with French wealth and magnificence. The cardinal seated his noble guest next to him, and, somewhat chagrined by his unbroken silence through the entire spectacle, at last asked what had most impressed him of all the remarkable things he had seen in France. "My lord," answered John de Wert at once, "nothing has so much astonished me in the dominion of his Most Christian Majesty, as to see ecclesiastics amusing themselves at theaters while saints languish in prison."

Great and general was the joy when, shortly after Richelieu's death, St. Cyran obtained his release.

D'Andilly went to bring him away in his carriage, and they drove once more through the forest of Vincennes. "No captive," says Mrs. Schimmelpenninck, "had ever received such demonstrations of esteem. His guards and fellow-prisoners threw themselves at his feet, to implore his parting benediction, and they mingled tears of joy at his release, with those of sorrow for his departure. His guards especially mourned his loss, and all the garrison, wishing to show their respect, spontaneously arranged themselves in two rows to let him pass out, to the sound of fifes and drums and discharges of musketry."

After a brief stop in Paris, they drove to Port Royal *des Champs*. But the good news was swallow-winged, and had reached the convent before them. It was the hour of silence when the announcement came—an hour strictly and solemnly observed by every member of the household. But Angélique could not keep her joy to herself. She hastened to the conference room, where the nuns were assembled, and her radiant face partly told the story. Then she snatched off the girdle which bound her robe, and held it out. The sisters guessed the parable, and tears of joy sprang to many eyes, and heads were bowed in thankfulness, though not a word was spoken. When d'Andilly and St. Cyran arrived, they went at once to the chapel, and the nuns, hastily assembled, sang a joyful *Te Deum* while their beloved father knelt at the altar to give thanks.

But the years of imprisonment and deprivation had produced their natural effect, and St. Cyran's health was permanently broken. He lived but a few months after his release. Through his illness he showed a sweetness of spirit worthy of his life. He was obliged to submit to a surgical operation, and, it is said, suffered much from the surgeon's unskillfulness. But he refused to call in another for three reasons. First, his life was in the hands of God and not of man, therefore it was no matter whether the surgeon was skillful or not. Second, the poor man was doing his best, and it would be unjust to punish him for what was not his fault. In the third place, the physician suggested was a personal friend of his own, whom it would be a great pleasure to see, and he wished to deny himself that gratification.

These three reasons are a good epitome of the man's character: Implicit faith in God; careful justice to his neighbor; no tenderness to himself.

# A HAPPY YEAR.

# VIII.

## A HAPPY YEAR.

THE "spiritual twinship" between Jacqueline Pascal and her brother had never been so strong as now.

They read the same books, they thought the same thoughts, they prayed the same prayers. They often wrote their letters to their sister in concert, using the "we" as naturally and freely as the habitual singular pronoun, and subscribing either both their names, or one or other of them, as it happened, apparently, and without any reference to the actual writer.

Some ideas and phrases found in the letters of this time are repeated in Pascal's celebrated "Thoughts," published twenty years later, while, by their side, like daisies growing in some temple porch, are the fresh, simple expressions of a young girl's feelings.

They were very free with one another and with their sister in speaking of their religious experiences.

Afterward they became much less so, owing to the extreme reserve recommended by the Jansenist writers as a safeguard against spiritual pride. "It seems to us," says one letter, "that, far from being forbidden, we are actually bound to make known to each other our joy over God's goodness to us as a family. We have a right now to consider our relationship as perfected; having before been united by the tie of flesh, we are now united in soul."

Their ardor in these early days is beautiful and inspiring to see. "There is no point," closes the same letter, "where it is not perilous for us to halt. We can only escape a fall by continually climbing higher."

The increasing feebleness of young Pascal's health must have deepened the tenderness of the intimacy between brother and sister. After he was eighteen years of age, he used to say, he never passed a day without pain. At times his maladies took on most distressing and alarming forms.

"Besides other annoyances," says Madame Perier, "he was unable to swallow any liquid unless it was lukewarm, and then only when it was trickled drop by drop down his throat." This was owing to a spasmodic action or partial paralysis of the throat.

"In order to relieve his intolerable headaches, his raging internal fever, and other ailments to which he was subject, his physicians ordered him to take certain medicines every alternate day for three months.

These all had to be swallowed in this tedious, lukewarm way. It was a veritable penance and pitiful to
see, but he never once complained."

Sometimes his limbs were paralyzed and he could
not move without crutches. His feet were cold and
heavy as marble, and in order to produce any circu-
lation in them, he was obliged to wear stockings
dipped in brandy.

Jacqueline during these days was housekeeper,
nurse, companion, friend—all that is meant by that
large word, *sister.*

Altogether, this year of her father's convalescence,
her brother's increasing need of her, of cheerful letters
back and forth between home and Clermont, and a
long visit from Gilberte and her husband at one time,
of household cares and activities—so many to the
mistress of a French family of the Pascals' station—
of growing interest in new lines of thought, and of
making acquaintance with new books to read—this
last year in quaint, bright, historic, inspiring Rouen—
seems to us the happiest year of Jacqueline Pascal's
life. Perplexing questions had not yet arisen. Life
was simple. Duty was plain. Sacrifice, if she was
conscious of any, brought with it, day by day, its own
reward. Her father, who, as Gilberte more than once
tells us, loved Jacqueline with " an extraordinary tenderness," was happy in the home she made for him.
Her brother was relieved by her ministries, soothed

by her sympathy, practically helped by her ready and interested assistance in his scientific pursuits.

Blaise was still at work on that vexatious little calculating machine. For though in theory it had long been perfect, its workmanship was so delicate and its principle so far above the comprehension of all the artificers he could find, that he had endless trouble in getting it into actual operation. He had not lost his childhood's love for geometry, and there are among his papers one or two undated fragments on mathematical subjects which were very likely written about this time.

But the principal subject of his investigations just now was the mechanical properties of the atmosphere, and he was considering with his usual keen and searching interest a series of experiments lately made in Italy on this subject.

We can not do more in this little book than stand on the border of that great region of physics in which Blaise Pascal delighted to roam. But, perhaps, if we linger there a moment we may, in some degree, share Jacqueline's sympathy with him.

It was the old theory of the " vacuum " which exercised his mind—a theory so old and so respectable that nobody for years had thought of calling it in question any more than we do that of gravitation. But it was an age of speculation and original investigation in science as well as in theology. And this, by the way, the historians of science inform us, is owing to Descartes, as great a revolutionist in his domain as Luther or Calvin had been in theirs.

When, therefore, it was found by the fountain-makers of Cosmo di Medici in Florence that water could be forced up in a tube only thirty-two feet, they began to inquire the reason of its refusal to go further, and consulted the aged philosopher, Galileo, on the subject. Antiquity had said: Water follows the piston up the tube of a pump because "nature abhors a vacuum." But why, asked the workmen, will it follow the piston only thirty-two feet?

For the honor of philosophy some answer must be given, and so Galileo answered that thirty-two feet was the limit of nature's abhorrence of a vacuum! Beyond that she did not abhor one.

Laughable as such an explanation may seem to us, it was received in all seriousness by those interested in the question then, and was, indeed, no more absurd than many an article of common faith in those days. But Galileo himself, it appears, felt somewhat uneasy as to the reasonableness of this dictum of his, and began to make experiments to prove it either true or false. He was an old man, however, and died before he had settled the point, leaving an earnest injunction to his pupil and successor, Torricelli, to carry on his investigations.

Torricelli did so, and published in 1645 an account

of his experiments, with the hint (for it was scarcely
more than that) that it was the *weight of the atmosphere*, and not the horror of a vacuum, which regulated
the height of a column of fluid in a tube. But he, in
his turn, died very soon after the publication of his
paper, and before his opinion was proved to be correct—"his suspicion really a secret of nature's"—kept
so well till now!

Our young philosopher at Rouen heard of these
things through Father Mersenne, a priest of scientific tastes, and an intimate friend of the great Descartes. And it was not long before Pascal's experiments "*touchant le Vide*" were as well known in
the world of science as Torricelli's.

He conducted them, as Torricelli had done, with
mercury, the heaviest known fluid, instead of water,
and the conclusion in his mind, also, was that the old
doctrine of nature's abhorrence of a vacuum had no
foundation to rest upon, and that all the phenomena
formerly explained by that were better explained by
the pressure of the atmosphere.

Early in this year, 1647, Blaise published a little
book giving an account of his experiments. The
Abbé Bossût assures us that not till after its publication did Pascal know that Torricelli's conclusions had
been the same as his own, though he had been informed in detail of the latter's experiments. However that may be, he simply makes in his book a plain

statement of his own observations and the natural inferences from them, and distinctly says that he makes no mention of what has been done in Italy, because, though he has repeated those experiments "in every sort of fashion," this is only an account of his own proceedings.

The Jesuits did not like this little book. And there were others who did not like it. "All the false science of the time," says Bossût, "arrayed itself against Pascal." He was accused of borrowing his ideas from the Italians, and (what was worse) of unsettling long-established beliefs. He was soon in the midst of a lively shower of controversial pamphlets. But he took wonderfully little interest in them. He was bent on discovering the truth, and proceeded calmly to devise some simple and final experiments which should forever settle the disputed point.

M. Pascal, the elder, however, thought it worth while to answer his son's most conspicuous antagonist, a certain Father Noël, Rector of the Jesuit College in Paris. He did so in a very strong and sarcastic letter—"une lettre de bonne encre," Sainte-Beuve calls it. Father Noël. in addition to several long letters of objections, had gone out of his way to write a poor burlesque, entitled "Le Plein du Vide."

M. Pascal makes unmerciful sport of the reverend gentleman's "figures of rhetoric which are not within the rules of grammar," but, above all, gives him to understand that, in dealing with his son, he is dealing with no common fee. "He is able to defend himself," closes the father's letter, "in terms capable of causing you an eternal repentance." This is strong language. But when Blaise himself began calmly to answer Father Noël's objections, taking them up one by one, and completely disposing of them, that gentleman, as we shall see, apparently thought there was a grain of truth mixed with paternal pride.

All these excitements, labors, and experiments, we are to remember, were carried on in the intervals of (or in the midst of) such distressing attacks of illness as Gilberte has described to us; in the midst, also, of constantly increasing attention to Church observances and religious duties, and of much reading of devotional books. •

Certainly every moment must have been fully occupied.

We can not help suspecting, with Sainte-Beuve, that Pascal's ill-health at this time—the tormenting headaches from which he suffered, and the terribly shattered condition of his nervous system—was partly owing to the mental struggle which began soon after his conversion. This was a conflict between his conscience and his thirst for knowledge—the two most powerful forces of his nature—and it would have been strange indeed if it had not made some impression on the sensitive physical frame.

One of the books which the good brother physicians had lent the Pascals during that winter of 1646, was a little discourse of Jansen's on the " Reformation of the Interior Man," and in it the ardent student read these cruel words:

" There is another desire worse than that of the senses; more misleading because it appears more honest. This is that always restless curiosity . . . . which has been palliated by the name of *science*. This makes the intellect its seat of empire, . . . . and the world is all the more corrupted by this malady of the soul because it is concealed under the veil of health, that is to say, of science. . . . . From this evil principle comes research into the secrets of nature which do not concern us, which it is useless to know, and which men wish to know only for the sake of knowing."

There are several pages more in the same strain, and we wonder if the good bishop did not mentally condemn himself, as he wrote them, for his own delight in digging out Hebrew and Latin roots!

But whatever the protests from Pascal's conscience, he, as yet, kept up his investigations with ardor and, as we have seen, with success.

In September of this year (1647) the brother and sister went to Paris, partly, it would seem, to seek medical advice for Blaise, and partly in search of recreation for him.

The young scientist's reputation brought him polite attention from many distinguished men, and Jacqueline mentions some of them in the following letter to Gilberte:

"MY VERY DEAR SISTER:—I have deferred writing to you because I wished to send a full account of my brother's interview with M. Descartes, and had not leisure yesterday to tell you that M. Habert called here on Sunday evening, accompanied by M. de Montigny, a gentleman of Brittany, and as my brother was at church, the latter informed me that his fellow-townsman and intimate friend, M. Descartes, had expressed a great desire to see my brother for the sake of the great esteem in which he and my father were everywhere held, and had requested him to come and see if it would be inconvenient to my brother (whom he knew to be an invalid) to receive a visit from M. Descartes the next morning at nine o'clock.

"When M. de Montigny made this proposal I was puzzled what to say, knowing the difficulty which Blaise finds in exerting himself or talking in the morning, and yet not thinking it right to decline the call. Finally it was agreed that M. Descartes should delay coming till half-past ten, and accordingly he came at that hour, in company with M. Habert, M. de Montigny, a young ecclesiastic whom I do not know, M. de Montigny's son, and two or three other youths. M. de Roberval, to whom my brother had sent word, was also there.

"After the usual civilities, the calculating machine was mentioned, and being displayed by M. de Roberval, was very much admired. They then began to discuss the theory of the vacuum, and M. Descartes, on being told of an experiment and asked what force he thought it was which expelled water from a syringe, said with perfect seriousness that it was *subtle matter;* to which my brother made what answer he could; and M. de Roberval, thinking that it hurt him to talk, took up the reply to Descartes with some warmth, though with perfect civility. But the latter told him, somewhat sharply, that he was willing to talk with my brother as long as they liked, because he spoke rationally, but not with him (M. de Roberval), for he was prejudiced.

"Then, perceiving by his watch that it was noon, and having an invitation to dine in the Faubourg St. Germain, he took leave; and so did M. de Roberval, who rode back with M. Descartes in a carriage, where, being quite alone, they sang merry songs and were rather wild; that is, according to M. de Roberval's account, who returned after dinner and found M. d'Alibrai here. I had almost forgotten to say that M. Descartes, sorry that he could only stay so short a time, promised my brother to come back at eight o'clock the next morning. . . . . .

"M. Descartes made this second call, partly to advise my brother in regard to his illness, concerning which, however, he said but little, merely recommending him to remain in bed every day as long as he could do so without weariness, and to take strong broths. They conversed on many other subjects, for he stayed till eleven; but I can not tell you what they were, for I was not present and could not inquire, having been very busy the rest of the day in superintending his first bath. He thought the bath made his head ache, but the water being too warm perhaps caused this. I think having his feet bled Sunday night did him good, for he was able to speak Monday quite forcibly, in the morning to M. Descartes, and in the afternoon to M. de Roberval, with whom he held a long argument on many points in theology and physics without any further inconvenience than a profuse night-sweat and wakefulness. I had feared a severe headache after so much exertion." . . . .

Another pleasant letter from Paris begins thus:

"We can not tell whether this letter is destined, like the other, to have no formal close, but we do know that when writing to you we never wish to leave off. We are now reading M. de St. Cyran's letter, *De la Vocation*, which was printed a short time since, and has given great offense. You shall have it as soon as we have finished, and we shall be glad to know your opinion of it and my father's also. Its tone is very high." . . . .

Descartes was not their only distinguished visitor. The Reverend Father Noël one day sent one of his Jesuit *confrères* to inquire kindly after his young adversary's health. He very much feared that the answer to his first objection (which had lately been published and widely read) might have been injurious to the writer. He begged him not to risk his precious health again; in short, not to answer him any more! It would be better to wait till they could argue face to face.

" I avow," writes Pascal to a friend, "I avow to you that if this proposition had been made to me by anybody but these good Fathers I should have suspected it! But I doubted their sincerity so little that I gave them my promise without reserve."

And after this the Jesuits accused him of having nothing more to say for himself against Père Noël!

The experiments went on, however, and told their own story. From the top of the Tour St. Jacques young Pascal conducted them in person, and triumphantly proved the theory of atmospheric pressure.* You may see his statue to-day in the vaulted

---

* Pascal's reasoning was this: If atmospheric pressure is the force supporting the column of mercury, then that column will diminish as you leave behind it successive layers of that weight. The column gradually fell in ascending the tower, and as gradually rose in descending, and thus proved his hypothesis correct. This

chamber at the foot of the beautiful tower, and many a reader of this page, doubtless, has seen it. This achievement alone would have made Pascal famous. Yet it is not for this that the world to-day chiefly does him honor.

To make assurance doubly sure, Blaise sent to his brother-in-law, M. Perier, to repeat these experiments at Clermont upon the Puy de Dôme, that being three thousand feet high, whereas the Tour St. Jacques was only a hundred and fifty. Here, also, they were brilliantly successful.

Bigotry and prejudice had nothing more to say, and the old doctrine of nature's abhorrence of a vacuum was dropped from the creed of science.

Among the choicest of their pleasures in Paris, Blaise and Jacqueline Pascal regarded the preaching of M. Singlin, whom they often heard at the church of Port Royal de Paris. Singlin was St. Cyran's successor as chaplain and confessor of the convent. He was a man of great goodness and wisdom, and one of the most distinguished preachers of the reformed or reforming party in the Church.

Through their own pastor, Guillebert, they obtained an introduction to M. Singlin and, in due time,

is simply the principle of the barometer, now so familiar. Full accounts of these experiments and their results are given in many lives of Pascal, and a very clear and interesting one in an article by Sir David Brewster in the *North British Review* for August, 1844.

to the Abbess Angélique and the other Port Royal celebrities.

And so this happy year draws to its close. We like to linger over it. It is a beautiful picture, and it ought to have lasted longer. We can not help regretting that what seem to us mistaken notions of duty should have so soon destroyed it. We can not help wishing that the idea of becoming a nun, which now presented itself to Jacqueline, had never entered her head. We wish she had thought it right—had *seen* it right—to let her light shine at home, and, however she might have treated the offers of marriage now coming frequently, we are told, had, at least, devoted her life to making a "sunshine in a shady place" for the father and brother who had been, and still were, so much to her.

What such a girl might have been, *at home*, to her own immediate family, to her nephews and nieces, to her servants and her poor, to the noble society which opened its doors so freely to her—how broadcast she might have sown her precious seed—how widely diffused the leaven of her sweet, pure life—it is impossible to estimate. And no student of her character can fail to feel that at this point Jacqueline Pascal made the mistake of her life. She sought too high the way of duty and missed the narrow, sweetly-shaded path at her feet.

Yet, even in our regret we are met by another

thought :—that, whatever the mistakes of a consci
entious soul, through those very mistakes, sometimes
by direct means of them, that soul is led into a higher
place.

Jacqueline Pascal had entered on a course of endless progress. She was going on. There was no
such thing for her as turning back.

As the brother and sister have shown us in that
happy letter of theirs quoted at the beginning of
this chapter, they had made up their minds "to
escape falls by continually climbing higher." They
chose a way to climb which certainly does not seem
to us the best way. But it brought them up! Was
the Lord going to let them fall because, out of love
for Him, they chose the steepest path?

They were entering into life. And if they must
pluck out the right eye or cut off the right hand and
enter into life maimed—so be it! Nevertheless,
they would enter in! It would have been nobler and
better to our thinking if they could have entered in
whole—a natural, beautiful, well-rounded man and
woman, as God created them to be.

A rose is at its best when, rich in all its crimson
beauty, it sends up its breath to heaven. But
crushed and beaten out of all its comeliness, a rose
still yields a rare perfume.

# CLIMBING.

# IX.

## CLIMBING.

SOME notion of the religious training of the Pascal family under Pastor Guillebert is given us in this passage from the " Memoirs of Margaret Perier," Gilberte's daughter :

" My father and mother, while at Rouen, were under the ministry of M. Guillebert, Doctor of the Sorbonne, a very holy and discreet man.   He counseled my mother, who was then twenty-six years old, to lay aside all her ornaments and wear no trimmings on her dresses, which she cheerfully did.   When she was obliged to return to Clermont, M. Guillebert told her that he had an important piece of advice to give her, and it was this : That ladies whose piety prevented them from wearing ornaments often took pleasure in decorating their children, and that she must be careful to avoid doing so, gay dress being far more injurious to children, who are naturally fond of it, than to grown persons, who, knowing its frivolity, care nothing for it. Accordingly, on her return to Clermont, where she had left my sister, then a little over four years old, and myself, then not quite three, she found that my grandmother, who had charge of us in her absence, had dressed us both in frocks embroidered with silver and fully trimmed with ribbons and laces, as was then the fashion. My mother took everything off and clad us in gray camlet without lace or ribbon. She forbade our nurse to let us play with two little girls of our own age in the neighborhood, whom we had been in the habit of seeing every day, lest we should acquire a love for the gay garments they usually wore. She was so particular on this point that, in 1651, when my grandfather Pascal died, and she was obliged to be present in Paris at the settlement of the estate, she chose to incur the expense of taking us with her for fear that my grandmother would make us dress in finer clothes, if we were left under her care. She always taught us to wear the most simple and modest clothing, and I can say with truth, that since I was between two and three years old I have never worn either gold, silver, colored ribbons, curls, or laces."

" Which she cheerfully did!" That is the key-note. Madame Perier, and, as we know quite well, Jacqueline and the whole family, are far too much in earnest to mind such trifles as these.

It is expected of them that they shall lay aside their ornaments, and they do so, as naturally and easily as some simple-hearted princess puts on her jewels, because *that* is expected of *her.* In either case the ornaments or the want of them are nothing.

Neither Gilberte nor Jacqueline ever allude to anything they have given up or write in a way that suggests sacrifice. It was not sacrifice to them. As Mrs. Charles has so well said in regard to another noble woman : " Not that she painfully denied herself luxuries. In the coinage of the kingdom where she dwelt they were simply valueless."

But when the question of giving up came to Blaise, then, indeed, it became a vital and a painful thing.

Those words of Jansen's which we have quoted are but a sample of what was to be found in many other of the best books of the day, and the young disciple heard on all sides the call to *sacrifice* mind and heart and soul and strength for Christ's sake and the Gospel's. The Roman Catholic Church has always regarded human nature not as a servant to be trained for the Master's use, but as a foe, to be subdued and crushed. There are other Christians who act upon the same theory. It is a terribly dangerous theory, for it results in the majority of men and women living in opposition to conscience, and nothing can be so blighting as that to all true growth of soul.

The struggle in Pascal's mind is evident in many ways. About this time he composed fifteen prayers for use in sickness. " Lord," he cries out in one of

them, " I know myself to be certain of but this one
thing. It is good to follow Thee. It is evil to offend
Thee. Beyond this I am ignorant of what is best or
worst for me." It is a glimpse into his secret heart—
perplexed and troubled, yet making sure of the one
main truth in which alone is safety.

The account of the atmospherical experiments was
followed quickly by two treatises on hydrostatics.
Then the physicians took sides with conscience and
forbade all scientific studies—forbade, indeed, all mental exertion—and there followed an effort at self-
annihilation more painful than all the struggles.
Surely, at this time, if ever, Blaise Pascal needed his
twin sister !

The brother and sister, apparently, never returned
to Rouen, for in May, 1648, M. Pascal was appointed
Councillor of State, and returned to make his home
in Paris.

During the winter they became better acquainted
with their new friends, and regularly attended church
at the convent chapel of Port Royal.

Port Royal was no common convent, as all of us
know who have read the lives of that noble band of
women who worked and worshiped within its walls.
" My sister came to the conclusion," says Madame
Perier, " that here, to use her own expression, one
might reasonably be a nun.

" She perceived from M. Singlin's preaching that

his ideas of a Christian's life were in accordance with those she had formed since God first touched her heart.

"She imparted her thoughts to my brother, who, far from dissuading her, encouraged her, for he was imbued with similar views. His approbation so strengthened her that thenceforth she never wavered in the design of devoting herself to God."

"My brother," Gilberte says again, "who loved her with especial tenderness, was delighted with her project, and thought of nothing but how he should aid her to accomplish it. . . . . My sister visited Port Royal as often as the great distance of her dwelling would permit, and the Abbesses told her to place herself under the charge of M. Singlin, in order that he might judge if she were truly called to a cloistered life. She did not fail to obey, and from the very first time that M. Singlin saw her, he told my brother that he had never known so strongly-marked a vocation. This testimony was a great comfort to my brother, and it made him doubly anxious for the success of a design which he had every reason to believe was of God. All this occurred in the early part of the year 1648, when my brother and sister were at Paris and my father at Rouen."

The brother's unselfish love comes out nobly here, and his genuine sympathy with the highest and best in his sister. True unity of spirit is that when each

can rejoice in the sacrifice the other makes! True
love is that which can allow the beloved one to renounce!

Because "he loved her with an especial tenderness," therefore "he was delighted with her project"
of dying to the world, to her home, to her youth, to
her fame, to himself forever. He was, in fact, one
with her in the matter; he saw it through her eyes
and felt it through her heart.

And Jacqueline herself? How was it with her?
Was there no conflict in her heart? Was there no
pain to her in this wrench from a life which had been
so pleasant and a home which had been so dear? It
can scarcely have been otherwise with such a girl as
she; yet we have no hint of any such thing. From
the first she seems to have thrown into this project
the same enthusiasm which she threw into her childish
play-acting and versifying.

It seems to have been Pleasure that beckoned, not
Duty that called. Her letters are full of it. She can
speak of little else, and she prays for grace to restrain
her ardor, not for grace to endure the trial. The
whole current of her desires, in fact, has changed its
course. She is filled, as Cousin says, with "an in-
vincible passion for solitude and the monastic life."

We have said there was no hint of a regret. There
is, among Jacqueline Pascal's collected verses, a little
poem, without date, which Reuchlin (her German

biographer) thinks must have been written about this time. He calls it the " Swan-song of the poetess ere she laid her gift on the altar of her God."

Here are the verses :

   ' O, ye dark forests, in whose sombre shades
      Night finds a noonday lair,
   Silence a sacred refuge ! to your glades
      A stranger, worn with care
   And weary of life's jostle, would repair.
   He asks no medicine for his fond heart's pain ;
   He breaks your stillness with no piercing cry ;
      He comes not to complain,
      He only comes to die !

   ' To die among the busy haunts of men  ·
      Were to betray his woe ;
   But these thick woods and this sequester'd glen
      No trace of suffering show.
   Here would he die that none his wound may know,
   Ye need not dread his weeping—tears are vain—
   Here let him perish and unheeded lie ;
      He comes not to complain,
      He only comes to die ! "

It is one of the prettiest poems she ever wrote, but it must always be a matter of mere conjecture whether Reuchlin's theory is correct. If this is an expression of her own feelings, certainly not another line of all she ever wrote, not a word of her brother's letters, or her sister's " Memoirs," or Margaret Perier's " Recollections," gives us any reason to think of her as, at any time, " worn with care," or " weary of life's jostle." Moreover, after the " Stanzas thanking God for recovery from the Small-pox," written in her childhood, there are none of her verses which have a personal bearing. They are all Sonnets, Songs, Serenades, To a Lady, To the Queen, to St. Cecilia, For an Album, etc., etc., according to the fashion of the day.

Many a girl of poetic temperament might easily find herself in the mood to write such a song as this, who yet would not wish to have it regarded .as an expression of personal feeling. And more than all, Cousin, who is probably Jacqueline Pascal's most thorough student and critic, makes no allusion to such a theory, and places the poem among those of earlier date.

In a nature like hers, it seems to us the internal strife would not have been heralded in verse; and if it had been, something like this would more likely have been her song:

> " Sweet is the smile of home : the mutual look
>     When hearts are of each other sure ;
>   Sweet all the joys that crowd the household nook,
>     The haunt of all affections pure ;
>   Yet in the world even these abide, and we
>     *Above the world* our calling boast ;
>   Once gain the mountain-top and thou art free,
>     Till then, who rest, presume ; who turn to look are lost." *

Whatever the conflict that did go on in Jacqueline

---

* " Keble's Christian Year."   First Sunday in Lent.

Pascal's heart, it was almost immediately forgotten—swallowed up—in victory.

Vinet, in a fine essay on her character, compares her Christian course to the military life of the great Prince of Condé, who leaped at once to fame by insisting on his own plans, against the advice of older generals, and carrying them out successfully in his first battle, Rocroy. " It is not the fate," says Vinet, "of every gallant spirit to begin its career with a Rocroy that shall at once put its greatness beyond the pale of doubt forever. What was Jacqueline Pascal's Rocroy? An internal victory witnessed by God alone, and owing more than half its grandeur to the clouds in which it was enshrouded. To annihilate self, and then to efface the most minute traces of that very annihilation—that was the task of this heroic girl."

And because her enthusiasm was the enthusiasm of victory, we see it lasting through her whole life and rising superior to every discouragement and obstacle. It was no mere short-lived ardor, the first warm outflow of a loving nature, gradually quieting and cooling as time went on. She had abundance of time to reconsider, as we shall see, and she had every encouragement to do so. But there is no evidence of a moment's shrinking from the life she had chosen. From her brother we have mournful confessions of a relapse into what he considered world-

6

liness, and Madame Perier's letters in later years show an occasional interest in earthly and secular matters. But in Jacqueline there is, from beginning to end, the same calm, equable flow of assurance of her high vocation and sacred joy in it.

In May M. Pascal arrived in Paris, and now it became necessary to inform him of Jacqueline's resolution.

Evidently everybody dreaded this duty. " M. Singlin thought he ought to be told," says Gilberte, and again, " My brother undertook to tell him. There was no one else who could." " The proposal," she continues, " surprised and strangely agitated my father. On the one hand, having begun to love the principles of a pure Christianity, he was glad to have his children like-minded ; but, on the other, his affection for my sister was so deep and tender that he could not resolve to give her up forever. These conflicting thoughts made him at first answer that he would see and think about it. But finally, after some vacillations, he said plainly that he would never give his consent, and even complained that my brother had encouraged the plan without knowing whether it would meet his approval. This consideration made him so angry with my brother and sister, that he lost his confidence in them, and ordered an old waiting-woman who had brought them both up, to watch their movements. This was a great restraint upon my sister, for she could not go to Port Royal except by stealth, nor see M. Singlin without some contrivance or dexterous excuse."

Here, then, was a sad state of things between this daughter, hitherto so faithful, and the father who "loved her with unusual tenderness."

But Jacqueline thought herself justified in secretly evading his will, though she would not openly disobey him. "Though under many restrictions she did not give up her occasional visits to Port Royal, nor her correspondence with its inmates, *which she managed with much tact !*"

Our fancy follows the plainly-robed figure, quickly threading the narrow streets of the old "Latin Quarter" for some brief appointment with her confessor, fearful, perhaps, at every corner, of meeting her father or seeing the face of the old waiting-woman peering at her from behind some little shop-window. She passes the Hotel Clûny, where a few years before she might have found the Mère Angélique and some of her nuns. She passes the Sorbonne, and it frowns upon her. At last she is "quite in the country" and stops before "a noble house with magnificent gardens." Church, school-house, infirmaries, storehouses, and offices cluster about it. This is Port Royal de Paris, now "La Maternité," one of the largest hospitals of Paris.

The dear Mothers Angélique and Agnes loved very

tenderly this warm-hearted young disciple.  Yet they
were far too true and upright to urge her coming to
them till she could obtain her father's full permission.

"I am as truly, dear child, your spiritual mother,"
says Angélique, "as if you were already within the
convent walls."   And Agnes writes to her: "You are
already a nun, my dear sister, because you have determined to obey the call which God has given you;
but you will cease to be one, if you wish to forestall
the precise moment of your profession which God
has put in His own power."   "It is your duty to follow God's guidance and to endure with meekness the
delays occasioned by His providence.   There is quite
as much sin in wishing to anticipate the will of God
as there would be in not obeying it at the proper
time."

Toward the end of this year, 1648, we find the last
of the joint letters from Blaise and Jacqueline to
their sister.   It is much too long to give entire, but
some extracts will serve to show its tenor:

"And now we have a little private scolding for
yourself.   What made you say that you had learned
everything in your letter from me?   For I have no
recollection of having spoken to you on the subject.
And were what you say true, I should fear that you
had learned the lesson in a wrong spirit, or you would
have lost the thought of the human teacher in think-

ing of God, who alone who can make the truth effectual. . . . . Not that we are to be ungrateful or forgetful of those who have instructed us when duly authorized, as priests, bishops, and confessors are. They are teachers and other men are their disciples. But it is very different in our case, and as the angel refused to be worshiped by one who was his fellow-servant, so we must beg you not to pay us such compliments again, nor to use expressions of human gratitude, since we are but learners like yourself." . . . .

" The perseverance of the saints is neither more nor less than God's grace perpetually imparted, and not given once for all, in a mass that is to last forever. This teaches us how completely we are dependent on God's mercy; for if He should for a moment withhold the sap of His grace we should wither away." . . . .

" Fear not to remind us of things we already know. They need to sink deeper into our hearts, and your discourse will be more likely to fix them there. And besides, divine grace is given in answer to prayer, and *your love for us is one of those prayers which go up without ceasing before the Throne.*"

M. Perier was at that time building a country-seat, which still stands at Bienassis, near the gates of Clermont. The brother and sister refer to it in this way:

"We have nothing special to say to you unless about the plan of your house. We know that M. Perier is too earnest in what he undertakes to be able to give full attention to two things at once; and the whole plan is so extensive that if he carry it out it must engross his thoughts for a long time. . . . . So we have advised him to build on a more moderate scale, and only that which is absolutely necessary. . . . . We beg you to think seriously of this and to second our advice, lest he should be more prudent and take more pains in the erection of a house which he is not obliged to rear than in the building of that mystic tower whereof St. Augustine speaks in one of his letters, which he is solemnly pledged to finish. Adieu.   B. P.——J. P."

Then follows a postscript by Jacqueline:

"I hope soon to write about my own concerns, and give you full particulars; meantime, pray to God for my success."   And after that a line in her brother's handwriting: "If you know any charitable souls, bespeak their prayers for me, too."   Poor Blaise! Another glimpse into his troubled heart!

By her "own concerns," Jacqueline, of course, means her plan of going into the convent. She let slip no opportunity of announcing her determination to take the veil, and, though yielding literal obedience to her father in not leaving his house, she thought it right to prove to him by her manner of life that she was immovable in her decision. If she could not be a nun at Port Royal, she would be a nun at home. Her sister says:

"The difficulties she met with did not lessen her zeal, and having renounced the world in heart, she no longer took the same delight as formerly in amusements. So that, although for a while she concealed her intention of devoting herself to God, it was easily perceived, and she then withdrew from society and broke off suddenly from all her acquaintance. For this a favorable opportunity was offered by my father's changing his residence. She made no acquaintances in her new neighborhood, and escaped from her old ones by never visiting them. Thus she found herself at liberty to live in solitude, which became so pleasant to her that she gradually retired even from the family circle, and sometimes spent the whole day alone in her chamber. It is impossible to say how she employed herself in this perfect solitude, but each day it could be perceived that she was visibly growing in grace."

Her determination was not without its effect on her father. Madame Perier says again:

"My father was well persuaded that she had chosen the better part, and parental tenderness alone made him oppose her project. Finding, therefore, that each day only strengthened her resolve, he told her that he saw plainly the world had no interest for

her, that he fully approved her design and would
promise never to listen to any proposals for her settlement in marriage, however advantageous, but that
he begged of her not to leave him, that his life would
not be very long, and that if she would only be
patient till its close, he would allow her to live as she
chose at home. She thanked him, but made no positive answer to his entreaty that she would not leave
him, promising, however, that he should never have
any reason to complain of her disobedience."

Some time after she had entered on this way of
life, the father, brother, and sister made a visit together at Clermont.

"She greatly dreaded this journey," says Madame
Perier, "because of the influx of relatives and company to which one is exposed in a little country
town, and accordingly she wrote me that in order to
avoid this probable embarrassment, she thought I
had better publicly announce her determination to
take the veil, and that her profession was only deferred out of respect for my father's wishes. I did
not fail to fulfill my commission, and it succeeded so
well that on her arrival no one was surprised to see
her dressed like an old woman, with great simplicity,
nor that after having returned the first calls of civility, she shut herself up, not merely in the house, but
in her room, which she left only to go to church or
to take her meals, and into which none ever intruded.

So that even in my own case, if I had anything to tell her, I used to make a little memorandum or some kind of mark, that I might remember it when she came to table or on our way to church, whither we always went together. This was my best opportunity of speaking to her, though very short, as we had not far to go. Not that she forbade me or any one else to enter her room, nor that she refused to listen, but that we saw whenever her thoughts were called off in order to talk on subjects not absolutely necessary, it evidently tired and wearied her so much that we tried to avoid giving her the annoyance."

This was the state of things in the family for the next three years, while M. Pascal appears to have been vibrating between Paris, Rouen, and Clermont, and Blaise was fulfilling, as best he could, that wise prescription of the doctors, to think of nothing, have no cares, and lead a happy life.

6*

# PORT ROYAL AND THE MÈRE ANGÉLIQUE.

# X.

## PORT ROYAL AND THE MÈRE ANGÉLIQUE.

PORT ROYAL is another of those charmed names of history. And it is worth noticing that its charm is simply the pure halo of goodness—goodness so thorough and direct that the world has called it heroism.

No famous battles, visible to the eye of flesh, were ever fought in that narrow valley of Chevreuse, and few stirring events took place there till the very last years of the convent's five centuries of life.

Neither is there anything imposing or strikingly beautiful in the natural features of the place. The nuns came to love it as we all love our homes, and some of them, in their letters affectionately refer to the peaceful, church-like vale, with its walls of wooded hills and its high, blue, starry roof.

But Madame de Sevigné, who looked at it through quite other, though not unfriendly, eyes, speaks of it as " un dêsert affreux." And in reality it was an ill-drained (rather an un-drained), marshy spot, full of confined and noxious airs, and owing its very name to the corrupt Latin word *porra*, which means "a hollow, overgrown with brambles, containing stagnant water."

This valley, the site of the original convent, known as Port Royal *des Champs*, lies about eighteen miles from Paris, on the road between Versailles and Chevreuse. From the restored splendors of Louis Fourteenth's court one may drive in about an hour to this neglected spot. There, a recent visitor tells us, "nothing of interest remains to-day but a ruined fragment of wall to which has been built a rough, shed-like structure, surmounted by a wooden cross." Under this shelter there have been collected a few portraits, among them those of Agnes Arnauld, Jansen, St. Cyran, Racine, and Pascal.

The history of Port Royal, from its foundation in 1208 till the close of the sixteenth century, does not concern us. It is but the common and painful story of many so-called "religious houses."

A convent in theory was a beautiful thing, a place where humility, chastity, poverty, obedience, self-denial, and charity prevailed. A convent in reality was often a place where unmarriageable women led lives as easy and, in many cases, as sinful as a very lax discipline would permit.

Under Angélique Arnauld the theory became the

reality, and if we first glance at her life and character we shall best read the true story of Port Royal.

The story of this noble and charming woman is more fascinating than many a romance. At seven years of age she finds herself a nun, at eleven years an abbess, while her little sister Agnes, six years old, takes the same office in the neighboring convent of St. Cyr. For the Arnaulds are a large family— twenty children in all—and something must be done with these little girls or there will not be marriage dowries enough for all.

Only ten of the twenty children lived to grow up ; but of these—six daughters and four sons—every one was famous. And as we shall meet some of them occasionally at Port Royal, a few words of introduction, just here, may not come amiss.

First in age came d'Andilly, so named from his estate, whom we may remember as the " friend *par excellence*" of St. Cyran. He was a noble, generous, talented man, full of winning qualities. He was very popular at court, and it was through his influence that many of the royal and noble converts to the truth were made. It was through him that the Duchess d'Aiguillon became interested in St. Cyran and visited him at Vincennes.

Next to d'Andilly came the eldest sister, Madame le Maître, in reference to whom Angélique, when a little girl, exclaimed, " Oh, how unlucky I am to be the second daughter, for if I had been the eldest, I should have been the one to be married!"

Madame le Maître's "luck," however, was but poor. Her marriage was anything but happy, and years afterward she came, only too gladly, to seek refuge in her sister's convent. She brought with her a humble, tender heart and a practical head, and was a great favorite in the house. Before she took the veil, and thus gave up all claim to her property, she obtained permission to visit all the offices of the convent and ascertain what was wanting in them. "My sisters," she said to the nuns, "tell me all your little wants, for before long I shall have nothing to give away." And then, like a good housewife, she set everything in order, and provided whatever seemed necessary for the comfort and convenience of the household.

Next on the family list come Angélique and Agnes, who were early disposed of as we have seen. Their grandfather, M. Marion, was a friend of the king, who conferred ecclesiastical dignities, and the pope's sanction was easily obtained by sending to Rome false certificates of the children's age. Nobody seems to have regarded this step as a particularly dishonorable one. "The king only laughed," we are told, "to think how his Holiness had been tricked." The children themselves, however, took the matter more seriously. When their grandfather informed them of their fate, Angélique "ran off into a long gallery, crying with vexation and anger."

"But," explained her grandfather, "I shall make you an abbess, *the mistress of all the others.*"

This promise consoled her a little, and she finally said: "Grandpapa, if you wish me to be a nun, I will be a nun; but not unless you make me an abbess."

'And I," said Agnes, "I am willing to be a nun too; but I don't want to be an abbess."

A few days later they were again in their grandfather's study, and the little Agnes spoke up: "Grandpapa, I have quite made up my mind not to be an abbess, for they say an abbess has to answer to God for the souls of her nuns, and I am sure I shall have quite enough to do to save my own."

"But *I* want to be an abbess," said Angélique eagerly, "and I shall take good care that my nuns do their duty and behave well."

The characteristics shown in this childish conversation remained with the sisters through life. Angélique was born to command—to lead other souls with her own "to glory and virtue." Agnes was timid, shrinking, and though full of charity and good works, much occupied with her own growth in grace.

Henri Arnauld was the next child, and he became famous as bishop of Angers and Cardinal Mazarin's ambassador at the Papal Court.

Then comes "Sister Anne," of whom we shall see more as Jacqueline Pascal's predecessor in teaching the convent school, and after her, Marie Claire, the one whose struggle against St. Cyran's influence we have recorded.

A valiant soldier, Simon Arnauld, is the next child, and next to him the pretty Madeleine, of whom St. Francis de Sales predicted when she was a child that she would become a nun if her mirror did not stand in the way. It did not stand in the way. At fifteen she became a novice, and in due time entered the sisterhood at Port Royal.

The twentieth and last child was Antoine, known as the "great Arnauld." He was twenty-four years younger than his eldest brother, d'Andilly, and his nephew Le Maître was some years older than he. It would take a volume merely to mention all that this great man did and all that he wrote in the cause of Jansenism and of theological truth as he viewed it. He worked hand in hand with Blaise Pascal, and the two were devoted friends, though not agreeing on all points.

Let us notice, in passing, that the paternal grand-father of all these Arnaulds—not the one who ob-tained the abbacies—was at one time a Huguenot. "He was led away into the error of Calvinism," say the annals, "but after a time God opened his eyes, though this can not be said with regard to several members of his family."

And now we must come back to our young An-gélique. Very pretty are the legends of the child-abbess, marching with white robe and uplifted crozier at the head of her nuns, receiving in the convent garden the homage of the king, Henry Fourth, rebuking the familiarity of the courtiers, and altogether making an edifying exhibition of infant piety.

More touching, because more true, is the tale of her girlhood, when she awoke to the reality of her position—the bitter irksomeness of her duties—the longing for freedom—the conscientious chafing under false vows. At one time, in despair, she nightly studied over her chances of escaping to her Huguenot aunts at Rochelle, and talking over the whole subject with them. "Oh, if she had only done that," we are inclined to exclaim, "what a new light might have been shed upon her path!" Yet, if she *had* done that, what a beautiful chapter of faith and love and courage and purity in the midst of corruption would have been lost to history! The Lord who was leading her led her aright!

After giving up this plan of escape, there came a strong-willed effort to make her life endurable by the study of Greek and Roman history, "Plutarch's Lives," and other not too secular subjects; then a long illness, brought on by mental conflict, and at last, one summer evening, after listening to the preaching of an itinerant Capuchin friar (who soon after became a Huguenot), she suddenly found, in complete surrender to her Lord and to His work, a fuller and a sweeter liberty than she had ever sighed for.  Henceforth she becomes the Mère Angélique indeed, and at seventeen begins her career as reform-. er; first of her own convent, and afterward, by order of her ecclesiastical superiors, of many others through-out France.

Angélique's life, as given in the " Memoirs of Port Royal," is a series of delightful anecdotes.  It is al-most impossible to classify them, fot is she not a woman?—a bundle of contrarieties?—but each one reveals some brave or tender trait.  How high-spir-ited she is,—how independent, — how unyielding when her will is fully set to do that which she thinks right!  In the early days of her reforms there was abundant need for this strength of will.

Her hardest task was probably her very first.

The original rules of her convent allowed inter-course with visitors only through the grating of the convent parlor, and so the father, mother, brothers and sisters who had regarded Port Royal almost as a second home, must be excluded.  A whole long day the contest went on between a father indignant and argumentative by turns, a grieved and weeping mother, d'Andilly angry and sarcastic, and Anne and Marie Claire astonished and speechless—all these on the one side, and this pale, slender girl of eighteen on the other.  She carried her point, but she fell fainting the moment it was gained.

Through life the same strength and decision were hers, and in her seventieth year she speaks with compunction of her "brusque, imperious nature and habit of command." One day a visiting nun from Poissy told how in her convent they had cut off part of the chants as a mortification. "Much better have cut off the tails of your gowns," was the quick retort from the aged abbess, who had always hated nonsense. And in her very last days a box on the ear was not too severe a punishment for a foolish nun who tried to make out that the reverend mother had miraculously caused some heavy bread to become light.

Yet how tender she was!—how thoughtful in her tenderness! There was a certain Sister Marguerite, who caused the abbess much trouble, and in the end proved incorrigible. After a violent outbreak of temper, Angélique would not allow her to partake of the Holy Communion, and, in anger at this, Sister Marguerite ran away. The abbess and her nuns fasted many days, and prayed that the Lord would have mercy on the wanderer and restore her to them, and at length she was sent to them from a convent in Paris. It was evening when she arrived, and when Angélique heard the carriage wheels, she had all the lights put out, so that no one might see the penitent in her humiliation. She stood alone at the open door, took Sister Marguerite in her arms and kissed her, and "Oh, my dear child!" were all the words she said. .

Though strict in requiring renunciation where she thought it a duty, the Mère Angélique would not allow unnecessary discomfort. On chilly mornings, after matins (at four o'clock), she would with her own hands make a fire and insist on every one going to warm herself. She often visited the kitchen and tasted the food, to be sure that it was palatable. The cook, at one time, was a lay-sister of another order of nuns, and ate no meat. The consequence was that her own dinner, unless she prepared one especially for herself, was apt to be poor, and the abbess, suspecting this, followed her one day to the refectory and saw what she was about to eat—the scraps left from the last convent fast-day. Angélique brought some eggs, beat them up and made an omelette, saying to her lay-sister, as she set it before her, that whenever she neglected to provide a dinner for herself, the thing would be repeated. The cook was filled with confusion at being waited on by her Lady Superior, but she could not help laughing as she declared it was the best omelette she had ever eaten.

Great was this woman's faith! At one time she wanted three hundred francs to send to the farm at Port Royal *des Champs*, six hundred for another convent, a hundred and fifty to pay a debt, and two hundred for the butcher. "I had not a single sou," she writes, "so I went to my room and prayed to God for the money, and when my prayer was ended, a widow lady came to me, and said she had changed her mind as to the disposal of two thousand three hundred francs she had laid by, and instead of keeping them herself, she wished to give them to me for our immediate use. And after this, people tell me to ask alms of man and not of God! Indeed I shall ask God! I shall always beg from God and not from man!"

During the civil wars in 1652, manufactures were suspended, and the common serge worn by the nuns of Port Royal became very difficult to procure. A few pieces of greatly inferior quality had remained unsold from previous years, and these were now offered for sale at war prices—nearly double the former price of the good article.

M. Guais, who acted as the Mère Angélique's agent in such matters, had been asked to try to find some serge, but he was unwilling to buy so poor an article at so high a price, especially as the convent was just now low in funds. He was, therefore, delighted one day at finding some *Ras de Nord*, a very beautiful and durable material, which, by some chance, he could get at a very low price. He bought a piece at once and sent it to Port Royal, confidently expecting an order for more. But Angélique wrote back, " I would much rather buy the common stuffs, at double the price, than suffer these fine ones to enter the community. I consider the money I shall pay not in the light of a dear price paid for an article of dress, but as a cheap price to keep vanity and finery out of a religious house." "Things are not always to be estimated at the money they cost. That must ever be a dear purchase which is at the price of Christian simplicity." Since, however, the unlucky M. Guais had bought one piece, she decided to keep it, but it was all cut up into stockings, where its beauty could do no harm !

Dear saint ! Notwithstanding her precautions the annals of the convent show now and then a loophole for feminine vanity. Even the reverend Mother herself is said to have had one weakness—a large yellow patch on her white gown, which she contemplated with immense satisfaction. "Patches," she used to say, "are a nun's jewels."

This genuine love of "sacred poverty" is one of Angélique's strongest characteristics. Money, to her mind, was simply and absolutely a means to an end. Millions of francs passed through her hands, for at one time Port Royal was very much the fashion, and court and nobility lavished gifts upon it. But the wish to possess any of this money—the desire to own even a book or a relic, seems to have been unknown to her. Everything was absolutely in common, and even St. Francis' letters, her greatest treasures, she regarded as the property of the convent. Avarice she speaks of as a "curious" passion. She can not understand it.

"It is scarcely credible," say the "Memoirs," "how many families, both of the poor and of the reduced gentry, were relieved during the civil wars by the bounty of Port Royal."

The embroidery and fancy-work common among nuns were an abomination to Angélique, but the sisters were taught, with infinite patience, economy and neatness, to repair their own garments, and to make up into clothing for the poor every available remnant and scrap. Nothing was too sacred for use in charity. The gold and silver candlesticks of the church service were more than once sold for the benefit of the poor, and the very napkins off the altar torn into bandages for the wounded.

There was a permanent infirmary within the convent gates where women and children were nursed and medicines were dispensed. With her own hands the reverend Mother would strip off their rags, wash, clothe, and tend them. She was by nature skillful in all woman's work, and had the cheerfulness, tact, and presence of mind in the sick-room that are the sure signs of a good nurse. No disease, however loathsome or infectious, dismayed her, and she learned to use the lancet as well as a surgeon.

It was in such service as this that Angélique and her nuns passed their days, and in this way they manifested their piety. "Perfection," the dear Mother often said, "consists not in doing extraordinary things, but in doing ordinary things extraordinarily well." "Neglect nothing," again she would say. "The most trivial action may be performed to God. Even in rising to matins, be careful to make no noise, lest you disturb·invalids; if Christian charity be in your heart your whole life may be a continual exercise of it." "Oh, if we did but love others how easily the least thing, the shutting a door gently, the walking softly, speaking low, not making a noise, or the choice of a seat so as to leave the most convenient to others, might become occasions of its exercise." Truly, we are inclined to say with Jacqueline Pascal, "at Port Royal one might reasonably be a nun."

One secret of the Mère Angélique's success was her quick insight into character. One day four candidates were ushered into the convent parlor. The abbess, as they entered, watched them closely, and whispered to the nun who sat by her, "That little one at the back is the only one that will stay." And she did stay, while the others, after due probation, were sent home.

Another secret of her success was her fine tact. A querulous and troublesome nun was once confined by illness to the infirmary where the abbess herself, on account of some indisposition, was also spending a few days. They were once left quite alone and unattended for some time, and the nun took occasion to remark that it was very provoking of the sisters to leave their reverend mother so long. "Oh, no," said the abbess, cheerfully. "It is good for me to be left. You know sick persons so easily slide into self-indulgence. Think how many single ladies, of rank and expectations far above mine, are, perhaps, through misfortune, at this moment destitute of any attendance. Many are thankful and happy in having only one little maid to do everything for them, and while she is out on business they must be left alone. So, my dear daughter, when we call and nobody answers, let us fancy that the little maid is gone to market, and wait patiently till she returns." The pleasant words were not forgotten, and when the sister afterward felt inclined to complain, she would say, laughingly, " My mother, the little maid is gone to market."

It is impossible in a chapter to do anything like justice to Angélique Arnauld. The records of her in the various Memoirs of Port Royal are an " embarras du richesse," and we can but gather up a few fragments. We can give but a line to her well-trained intellect—to the wisdom of her counsels to the Jansenist leaders—her clear-sightedness in regard to the movements of their Jesuit persecutors—the force of her few published writings—the charm of her familiar letters. Altogether, her character is like some many-sided crystal—sparkling, whichever way we turn it. She is one of the Lord's own jewels. And through each clear-cut facet shines the same pure Light.

# AT THE CONVENT GATES.

# XI.

## AT THE CONVENT GATES.

IT is easy to see how with such a woman at its head, or rather, at its heart, Port Royal became the nucleus of the reforming party in the Church. Angélique Arnauld was, indeed, in its early days, the leading spirit of that noble band—that "fountain of sweet waters in the midst of the brackish sea." Gladly enough, however, she gave place to her revered spiritual father, St. Cyran, and when he was gone and she was beginning to feel the burden of years, her young brother and Pascal, her nephews, and hosts of friends were ready to step into the front ranks.

While Jacqueline Pascal was still a little girl, the nuns had moved from the valley of Chevreuse to Paris. Port Royal had become so popular that the house was too small for the many applicants for probation. "Besides," say the chronicles, "the situation became exceedingly damp and unhealthy. The whole monastery was continually enveloped in a thick fog. The house at length became a complete infirmary. Deaths constantly succeeded each other; yet numbers of fresh postulants were perpetually offering."

Madame Arnauld was now a widow, and her six daughters urged her to come and be a nun with them. She was a woman of lovely Christian spirit, but up to this time had naturally not felt herself called to the life of the cloister, having been married at fourteen and occupied with the care of her twenty children. She laughed when the proposition was first made to her, and said: "How can I begin to learn obedience at fifty, when I have been exercising authority since I was fifteen?" But she finally decided on the step; first, however, buying "a noble house with magnificent gardens" in the Faubourg St. Jacques, employing one of the first architects of the day to build a church attached to it, and bearing the expenses of the removal from Port Royal *des Champs* to Paris.

It was a few years after this that some of St. Cyran's disciples, prominent among them Angélique's nephews, the Le Maîtres, withdrew from the world into profound retirement, gave up their lives to worship and charity, and became known as Recluses. The little house which they took in Paris soon proving too small for their increasing numbers, "they determined to go to Port Royal *des Champs* and take possession of the convent the nuns had abandoned.

There they found everything bearing marks of the most complete desolation. The lakes, for want of draining, were converted into noxious marshes, over-grown with reeds and other aquatic plants ; they continually exhaled the most pestilential vapors. The grounds were in many parts completely overflowed. The gardens were not only overgrown with weeds and brushwood, but the very walks were infected with venomous serpents."

" The hermits, however, were not to be deterred by trivial inconveniences. Many of them were young men of the first families in France, yet they did not disdain to labor with their own hands. The little company set joyfully to work, and the aspect of the valley was soon transformed. The surface of the swampy morass soon exhibited a clear lake, whose waters re-flected the hills around, crowned with thick forests of oak. The tangled brushwood was felled. The spacious gardens blossomed as the rose, and the (rebuilt) walls of Port Royal arose from the ground amidst hymns of prayer and shouts of praise.

" New associates were continually quitting the world and joining themselves to this little band. After a short period it became a numerous and flourishing society. Regular plans and an orderly distribution of employments were soon found necessary."

" The Recluses of Port Royal, unlike religious orders, were not bound by any vows. Each, never-

7*

theless, sought to imitate his Lord, and follow His
steps, by a life of voluntary poverty, penance, and
self-denial.   They assumed the dress of no particular
order; yet they were easily distinguished by their
coarse and plain, but clean clothing.   Their time was
divided between their devotions to God and their
services to men.   They all met together several times,
both in the day and night, in the church.   Twice
each day, also, the whole company met in the refectory.   Some hours were occupied by each in his own
cell, in meditation, in private prayer, and in diligently reading and comparing the Holy Scriptures,
which they always did in the attitude, as well as in
the spirit of prayer, and to which exercise they devoted a portion of time every day.   Their directors
always advised them to begin by studying the Holy
Scripture itself, without any commentary, seeking
only for edification."

But as years went on over these recluses and over
Angélique's sisterhood in the city, that "noble
house" in turn became too strait for its occupants.
It became necessary to divide them, and send part of
the number back to the valley of Chevreuse.   How
they came back we will learn by again quoting from
the "Select Memoirs."

"The news of the nuns' intended return was soon
spread at Port Royal.   The whole neighborhood
evinced the greatest joy.   It was delightful again to
see them after so many years of absence.

" The recluses made every exertion to prepare the house and gardens. They put them in the best order for their friends. Their own books and furniture were soon packed up. On the morning of the very day the nuns were expected, they removed from the monastery. They took possession of a farm-house (Les Granges) which was situated at the top of the hill." "The Mère Angélique came in person to establish the nuns in their former habitation. On the day she was expected all the poor flocked to the monastery in their best clothes. As soon as the long file of carriages appeared through the woods at the top of the hill, they went to meet her. The bells were immediately rung; shouts of joy and exclamations of pleasure resounded on all sides. The procession stopped; then the poor with tears implored their good mother's benediction. She tenderly embraced them. At the church door she was met by all the recluses. They led the nuns into the choir, and after service, left them in possession of the convent and retired to their new habitation."

" The nuns and recluses never saw each other but at church; even there a grate separated them; nor had they any intercourse, though so nearly related, except by letter. . . . . The recluses continued all their former occupations; they conducted the farms and gardens and performed every other laborious office."

Under the wise care of these kind friends and brothers, and by means of the princely gifts which about this time flowed into the convent treasury, Port Royal *des Champs* became a very different place from the malarious valley we have seen it. The farms were much improved and became very productive. "The stagnant waters were drained and formed into clear lakes abounding with fish. The fields, gardens, and orchards were assiduously cultivated and enlarged." The fruit of Port Royal, indeed, was celebrated for its extraordinary size and fine flavor, so much so, that when M. d'Andilly annually sent presents to the Queen Mother, Anne of Austria, Cardinal Mazarin used to call it " fruit bénit."

Such were the two houses of Port Royal when Jacqueline Pascal first became interested in the convent.

The Mère Angélique was not perpetual abbess of either house. One of her early acts of humility had been the securing of triennial elections for this office. But she was very frequently elected to it, as was also her sister Agnes. While they were still young girls, by the request of both sisters, Agnes had been allowed to give up the abbacy of her convent of St. Cyr and become a simple nun of Port Royal under Angélique. She had not lost her childish dread of the dignity, yet, after all, as we have said, she could altogether escape it.

The Mère Agnes is a very interesting character, though differing greatly from her sister. She was something of a mystic by nature, and would gladly have spent her life in perpetual adoration. Her favorite book in her youth was the Life of St. Theresa. She pored devotedly over its pages while Angélique was reading Plutarch's Lives.

One day while she was a novice she was carrying a can of oil to clean the choir lamps, and spilled it over her dress and on the steps of the church. Any other novice would have been greatly troubled at such an accident, but to the lips of Agnes rose the words, "Thy name is as oil poured forth." She meditated a few moments on her loving thought, but then humbly wiped up the oil and went to her sister, the young abbess, to confess her fault.

Angélique, though she had a great admiration for her younger sister, thought she was in danger of being led away by prayer and fasting from the practical work of life. One day as a "mortification" she sent for Agnes to come out of church, and she came "weeping bitterly." Many years afterward, when Agnes was abbess, Angélique said to her one day, "Ah, mother abbess, do you remember the day when I fetched you weeping from the choir, because you cared for nothing but prayer? It is forty years ago, but I am sure that if I were to keep you away from church now, you would weep as bitterly as you did then. Truly there is no cure for our old diseases."

Nothing is told us of the Mère Angèlique's personal appearance, but Agnes' sweet face is often spoken of. Among the few ornaments allowed at Port Royal was a large painting on the refectory wall, by Philip de Champagne, representing the Mère Agnes on her knees by the bedside of a sick nun, praying for her recovery. The prayer was granted, and the event gratefully commemorated in this way.[*]

Agnes Arnauld was the author of several little devotional books. One of these, " Le Chapelet Secret," had the honor of being condemned by the doctors of the Sorbonne and suppressed by the Pope. Another, the " Portrait of a Perfect and an Imperfect Nun," has been said to " display so much spiritual acumen, that if entitled, ' The Portrait of a Consistent and a Half-hearted Christian,' it would not be unworthy of a place beside the soul-searching treatises of her Puritan contemporaries."

It was the Mère Agnes who, for the most part, kept up the correspondence with Jacqueline Pascal during the latter's years of waiting outside the convent gates. Regularly every month a letter came, always full of affection, and usually of sound advice.

"Yesterday," runs one of them, "we had an admirable sermon from M. Singlin ; I could have wished you had been there, but for the fear that it

---

[*] Mrs. Jameson gives a sketch of this picture in her " Legends of the Monastic Orders."

might have excited your desire of taking the veil, and made your present state of suspense more painful."

Again, " If you do not possess your soul in peace and perfect submission, you must cease the repetition of the Lord's Prayer, for the phrase, ' Thy will be done on earth as it is in heaven,' includes the renunciation of every possible wish which does not harmonize with God's will. I do not believe, dear sister, that you can desire to have things arranged in any other way than as God chooses ; for a conventual life will not make you what He designs to have you become, unless you enter upon it in accordance with His will, and at the hour of His appointment."

And yet once more, " You are bound to accept the answer given you by your father as a decree of God, who sees fit to reserve some other season for the gracious fulfillment of those desires He has inspired within you."

Some of Angélique's wise instructions, taken down from her lips (by stealth, for the abbess would never allow it to be done with her knowledge), were copied and sent to Jacqueline. We must quote one passage, even at the risk of becoming wearisome :

" It may be said with equal advantage, both to the novice who has her profession to make and to the nun who has already made it on the best grounds, *examine your own hearts.* There is an indolent retirement from the world which arises from sloth; there is a selfish retirement, which originates in a misanthropic absorption in our own concerns; there is a melancholy retirement, which is grounded on disappointed self-love; and there is a philosophic retirement which has its basis in pride and contempt of others. Far different from all these is a genuine religious retirement. The Christian's seclusion is founded on a deep experience of the deceitfulness of his own heart; nor is it deserving of that holy name unless while he comes out from the world to wait in silence upon God, he also diligently labors, by his industry and talents, as well as in his prayers, to serve to the very uttermost even that secular society conscience has obliged him to quit."

All these counsels, and especially Agnes' exhortations to patience, were needed, for Jacqueline's great temptation during these years seems to have been to restlessness and chafing under her delay. Her enthusiastic temperament and her strong will submitted with difficulty to the hard duty of waiting. Probably the first great lesson of obedience, so strongly insisted on by Angélique in her government, was better learned by Jacqueline Pascal in that solitary room in her father's house than it could have been amid the congenial activities of Port Royal life.

Poor child! The picture of her in these days looks dull and colorless enough beside the pleasant scenes we have been considering. Madame Perier speaks of her " strict solitude, which she never quitted, unless necessity obliged her." "And to all this," she continues, " she added great bodily austerities. As we had but scanty lodging-room (she was then at Clermont), a partition had to be put up for her accommodation in a place where there was no chimney, at some distance from the other rooms. There she passed a whole winter, without allowing us to do the least thing for her comfort, nor would she be persuaded to come near the fire at meal-times, which made us all very uneasy. Her abstinence also troubled us; for though she partook of our ordinary food, yet it was in such small portions, that, being naturally very delicate, she lessened her strength and ruined her digestion, till when, at last, we insisted on her taking more nourishment, she was unable. Her vigils, too, were extraordinary; not that we knew their exact length, except as we perceived by the number of candles she burned, and by similar circumstances. Her admirable foresight led her to prepare for a conventual dress, which, differing as it does from the dress worn generally, troubles the body and so clogs the soul; and to guard against this, she accustomed herself as much as possible to its inconveniences. Her shoes were made very low in the heel; she wore no corsets, cut off her hair, and put on head-dresses that were larger and more embarrassing than a veil would have been."

It is very probable that if Jacqueline had been, at this time, under the direct care of the Mère Angélique, these practices would have been less rigid, for Angélique did " not approve of austerities and severe penance." She thought they tended to develop spiritual pride. We have already quoted her very frequent saying, " Perfection does not consist in doing extraordinary things, but in doing ordinary things extraordinarily well." And the words of St. Francis de Sales were often on her lips—that " piety is not self-mortification, but doing the will of God ;" and that " fasting, in accordance with one's own will, is often a temptation of the devil."

But Jacqueline Pascal was young and ardent. " She loved much." And doubtless, when she fell at the Master's feet and broke there her " alabaster box of very precious ointment," though she may have done it mistakenly and blindly, the service was accepted and blessed of Him. That it was indeed so, seems evident from the effect of this life upon her own heart. There is no trace of spiritual pride, nor does her breaking of home ties and neglect of home duties produce so narrow and selfish a habit of mind as we might fear. She was not idle or forgetful of others in her solitude. " After regularly reciting her offices," says her sister, " and after reading, which employed her closely, as she made extracts from the books she read, she spent the rest of her time in working for the poor. She made them thick woolen stockings, under-linen, and other small comforts, which, when finished, she carried herself to the hospital. It was occasion of wonder and edification that this entire separation from the world did not make her sour in manners and temper, *but on the contrary, she was always charmingly affable*, and ever ready to go out of doors on any charitable errand, as we many times on trial found.

"During this time I was often indisposed, and she would sit with me all day, without seeming in the least disconcerted. Several of my children had violent illnesses, and she nursed them with admirable kindness. Even when one of my little girls died of confluent small-pox, my sister attended her to the last, and though the illness continued a fortnight, she only went into her own room to repeat her offices, choosing for that purpose the child's intervals of ease, watching over her night and day with the tenderest care, and passing many nights without once lying down. When there was no more need of her charitable services in this case, she returned to her usual course in her chamber. . . . . Jacqueline took great pleasure in visits to poor sick people about the town, accompanying an excellent young lady who devoted herself entirely to the poor."

By their fruits ye shall know them! When vigils, fastings, and coarse, uncomfortable garments produce "charming affability," kindness, and tenderness, we need not be afraid of them. It is easy to cry out against the austerities and the restrictions practiced by many Roman Catholic Christians. It is easy for us to see the harm they do. But let us make sure that in throwing away these things we are putting something better in their place. Let us not omit these and also leave the other undone.

It is a pity to force the fruits of the Spirit by these unnatural, painful processes. But it is a greater pity still not to cultivate the fruits of the Spirit at all, and in our liberty to forget the very object of that liberty.

"The religion of gloom suppresses human nature," says Cousin with much force and justice. "But the religion of mere pleasure does worse. It degrades it."

# WAITING.

# XII.

### WAITING.

THESE years were stormy ones for the nation, and perhaps the vacillations of the Pascals between Clermont and Paris may have been owing to the unquiet state of things in the capital.

The new cardinal (Mazarin) was even less popular than Richelieu had been. Those who had admired that royal maneuverer saw in Mazarin only a feeble and unworthy imitator of him. The nobles hated him because he was a foreigner, and the people because his taxes were extortionate.

It is scarcely necessary to say that Anne of Austria, though nominally Regent, was a cipher in the government. She was completely under the influence of the cardinal, and it was thought that a secret marriage existed between them.

Meantime Louis Fourteenth was receiving an education which has been thus described: " The infant king's amusements were all of a military kind. He delighted in handling arms and in beating drums. His intellectual education was neglected, but much attention was paid to his physical development, and his natural vanity, egotism, and haughtiness were encouraged rather than checked by his mother and his tutors. The avarice of Cardinal Mazarin induced him to stint the allowance and equipage of the young monarch, who slept upon worn and ragged sheets and had a most unbecoming and insufficient wardrobe."

Certainly this gives little prophecy of his brilliant reign—"the Augustan age of France." But we are to remember that Louis Fourteenth's reign was brilliant, not from the mind and character of the king, but from those of his gifted subjects. The cruelty, despotism, and fearful grossness of morals during this reign, are facts with which everybody is familiar. "And yet," say Buckle in his "History of Civilization," "there are still found men who hold up for admiration the age of Louis Fourteenth. They are willing to forgive every injury inflicted by a prince during whose life there were produced the letters of Pascal, the orations of Bossuet, the comedies of Molière, and the tragedies of Racine."

This is wandering a little from Cardinal Mazarin, but we will come back to say that, one day in 1648— that summer after M. Pascal had joined Blaise and Jacqueline in the city—Paris awaked to find itself in the hands of the mob. The cardinal had caused the arrest of two men who had resisted the taxes, and this was the result. The Swiss guards, stationed at the Tuilleries, were dispersed, barricades were erected in all the streets adjoining the palace, and the court, thus hemned in and defenseless, was obliged to repeal for the moment the obnoxious taxes.

This was the beginning of " the wars of the Fronde," so called from the epithet *frondeurs* (slingers) applied to the insurgents.

These wars soon became a mere series of intrigues between the nobility and the cardinal, and are far too intricate for us to follow. It is worth our while, however, to notice that that beautiful and accomplished woman, the Duchess of Longueville, at first took the lead of the party opposed to the court and cardinal, and thus placed herself in opposition to her brother, the great Prince Condé. A few years later she became a very different woman, and gladly left the tumult of the world for the cloisters of Port Royal.

During all the remaining years with which our little history has to do, these commotions or others similar to them were raging.

Paris was besieged by Condé in 1649, and all the surrounding country was involved in the distress of the city. The Mère Angélique writes from Port Royal *des Champs*: " We are all occupied in contriv-

ing soups and pottage for the poor.  This is, indeed,
an awful time.  Our gentlemen, as they were taking
their rounds yesterday, found two persons starved to
death, and met with a young woman on the very
point of killing her child because she had no food for it.

"All is pillaged around; corn-fields are trampled
over by the cavalry in presence of the starving own-
ers; despair has seized all whose confidence is not in
God; no one will any longer plow or dig; there
are no horses left, indeed, for plowing, nor, if there
were, is any person certain of reaping what he sows;
everything is stolen.

" Perhaps I shall not be able to send you a letter
to-morrow, for all our horses and asses are dead with
hunger.  Oh, how little do princes know of the de-
tailed horrors of war!  All the provender of the
beasts we were obliged to divide between the starving
poor and ourselves.  We have concealed, in our convent, as many of the peasants and their cattle as we
could, to save them from being murdered and losing
all their substance.  Our dormitory and the chapter-
house are full of horses.  We are almost stifled from
being pent up with these beasts.  But we could not re-
sist the piercing lamentations of the starving and
heart-broken people.  In the cellar are concealed
forty cows.  Our court-yards and outhouses are packed
full of fowls, turkeys, ducks, geese, and asses.  The
church is piled up to the ceiling with corn, oats, beans,

and pease, and with caldrons, kettles, and other things belonging to the cottagers. Every time we enter the chapel we are obliged to scramble over sacks of flour and all sorts of rubbish. The floor of the choir is completely covered with the libraries of our gentlemen.

"Thirty or forty nuns, from other convents, have also fled here for refuge. Our laundry is thronged by the aged, the blind, the maimed, the halt, and infants. The infirmary is full of sick and wounded. We have torn up all our linen clothes, and used all our rags, to dress their sores. We have no more, and are now at our wits' end. The cold is excessive, and all our fire-wood is consumed. We dare not go into the fields for any more, for they are full of marauding parties. We hear that the Abbey of St. Cyran has been burnt and pillaged. Our own is threatened with an attack every day. The cold weather alone preserves us from pestilence. We are so closely crowded that deaths take place continually. God, however, is with us, and we are in peace. I did not intend to tell you all this, but my heart is so full that I have written on without knowing it."

While she waited for the fulfillment of her vows and of her hopes, Jacqueline Pascal's mind was not stagnating, nor was her pen altogether idle, though she appears to have spent more time in copying and paraphrasing the writings of others than in original composition.

Of course the character of her productions is very different from that of earlier days. Her thoughts were deeper, higher, and undoubtedly the excellent models she so faithfully studied had their natural effect on her style, so that we find in her compositions after this time a certain elevation and dignity added to the gracefulness of her youth. "Her prose," says Cousin, " is always of the best quality, healthy, natural, ingenious, agreeable." Some of her "reflections" were considered so fine that it was once proposed to incorporate them with an edition of her brother's " Pensées," but this plan was given up, and they were added to the " Conferences of the Rev. Mère Marie Angélique Arnauld."

Jacqueline Pascal never attained the keen, clear thought and transparent style of her brother, but she belongs, as some one has said, to the noble order of the " *sisters* of genius," capable of appreciating the highest and best in another, and by her enthusiasm and her nobility of character, of inspiring that other to his greatest successes. Such a power is to most women a more useful and a more welcome gift than genius itself.

There are three papers written by Jacqueline, between the years 1648 and 1652, which are worth our attention. The first in time is a letter to her father, written soon after his refusal to her request, and before she had entered upon the strictly solitary life her sister has described to us. It is very long, taking up seven pages of Cousin's volume, and we can make but a few extracts from it. Her object in writing is to beg her father's permission to make a " retreat " of a fortnight at Port Royal, and very skillfully she makes her plea. She begins thus:

" MONSIEUR MON PÈRE:—As ingratitude is the blackest of vices, all that approaches it is so horrible that it can scarcely be thought of by one who has any love whatever for virtue. Forgetfulness of benefits received from another, above all when those benefits have been great and long continued, is ordinarily an effect of ingratitude, and want of confidence in this same person must be the effect of this forgetfulness. Therefore, I should believe it to be a crime to fail to *have great confidence in you on this occasion*, although, at the same time, I very much wish what I ask, and, ordinarily, those who wish fear also.

" First of all, I beg you, my father, not to be surprised at this request of mine, for it does not militate in the least against your will in regard to me as you have testified it. I also beg you, by all that is most holy, *to remember the prompt obedience* I have rendered you in that thing which touches me nearest of anything in the world, and the accomplishment of which I wish so ardently. Doubtless you have not forgotten this exact submission. You appeared too well satisfied with it to let it so soon pass out of your

mind.    God is my witness that I believe I have done
my duty in acting thus, and I only remind you of it
that you may understand that all my principles lead
me to undertake nothing important without your
consent.    After that, my father, I have no more
doubt that you will do me the honor to believe me
and to grant my request."

And now she fears she has gone too far and injured
her cause by making too much of it.    She changes
her tactics:

"After all this preparation you will think it is some
great request.    *It really is not that at all;* indeed, it
is so little that I believe I might have done it without
offending you in the least, if I had said nothing about
it !" . . . .

" Know then, my father, if you please (and, indeed,
I think you already are aware of the fact), that it is
a frequent thing among persons of all conditions,
whether living in the world or not, to make at certain
times, as their spiritual director may advise, two or
three weeks of retreat in some religious house, where
they enter into perfect seclusion, by permission of the
superior, and hold converse only with God and those
who are His.    Those who are most careful of their
salvation place themselves when they can in the best
regulated house they know of.    I think you see my
design, and I am sure you think with me that I can
not do better than choose Port Royal de Paris, nor

take a better time than that of your absence when I can render you no service.  Neither am I needed by any one else in the house, for since you went away I have not written a single word for my brother, and that is the thing for which he needs me most.  But he can do very well with some one else; indeed, I see no way in which I can possibly be needed until your return from Rouen, certainly if you compare such usefulness with the *necessity* which there is for my making this retreat."

And then, presently, she thinks of another good argument to urge: "For since God has shown me the grace to increase daily within me the effect of that vocation He has pleased to give me, and you have permitted me to keep, and which it is my desire to accomplish as soon as He shall make known to me His will by yours—since, I say, this desire augments every day, and I see no power on earth that can prevent my accomplishing it if you will and permit it—*this retreat would serve to prove whether it is there that God would have me.*  I could then listen to Him alone (*seul à seul*), and *perhaps I shall find that I am not born for that sort of place;* and, if it is thus, I will ask you frankly not to think of it any longer, or pay any more attention to what I have said to you. . . . . .

"Behold, *M. mon père*, the very humble prayer I make you.  I doubt not you will grant it. . . . . If I have ever been so happy as to satisfy you in anything, I beg you grant me promptly what I ask. The abbesses, on their part, have accorded me the privilege. M. Perier, my brother, and *ma fidèle* (Gilberte), approve my plan and are quite willing, provided I can gain your consent. . . . . .

"If there were any other consideration stronger than the love of God, which will urge you for His sake to accord me this slight request, I would employ it. In the name of that sacred love which He gives to us, and which we owe to Him, grant this request, *either to my weakness or to my arguments.* . . . . .

"You may be certain that your commandments are laws to me, and that where your satisfaction is concerned, even at the prejudice of my whole life's repose, I promptly hasten to obey. It is gratitude and affection rather than duty that leads me to do this, and when I accord to you what you demand of me, it is from pure love to your service next to that of God. This service is the reason you have given for keeping me with you. I hope in God you will some day know how much better I could serve you by being with Him than by being with you. But while waiting for this time, I pray Him to keep me in the same sentiments I have always had, to await patiently your will after I have sought to discover His.

"On the subject of my little retreat I await your answer with impatience such as you can imagine, but

with entire submission, *although I have the greatest
desire for it.* Whatever your answer may be, it will
not in the least change the passion it will find in me
—a passion which will never leave me—of proving to
you how much more I am by the affection of the
heart than by the necessity of nature, M. my father,
your very humble and very obedient daughter and
servant, JACQUELINE PASCAL.

" M. Perier, my brother, and *ma fidèle*, humbly kiss
your hands."


A better specimen of a woman's logic—compounded
of tenderness, obedience, defiance, pleading, argument, and religion—it would be difficult to find. It
is easy to recognize in the writer the little girl who
sat on Richelieu's knee, and through tears and caresses, backed by genuine determination and a fine
talent for sticking closely to the point, obtained her
father's pardon.

We are not told whether this letter brought the
desired permission, but it certainly deserved to do so.

While Jacqueline was at Clermont, living in the
little cold room partitioned off for her, making " coats
and garments " and taking them to the hospital, she
became acquainted with a certain good Father of the
Oratory, who seems to have been much interested in
the earnest young disciple. Madame Perier says:

" The good man often came to see my sister, and
8*

his edifying conversation gave her pleasure. He one day said to her that, since her talents had formerly been employed on worldly themes, it was but reasonable that she should now use them in some attempt at honoring God; that he had heard of her as writing poetry, and had thought of furnishing her with an opportunity of thus glorifying God by translating for her some of the Church hymns from Latin into French prose, which she might afterward versify. She replied promptly that she was quite willing. He brought her first the Ascension hymn, *Jesu, nostra redemptio,* which is chanted every day at the Oratory, and she put it into rhyme."

This hymn is supposed to have been written by St. Ambrose in the year 390. It is given us in some of our church collections as follows:

> "O Christ! our Hope, our heart's desire,
>     Redemption's only spring;
>   Creator of the world art Thou,
>     Its Saviour and its King.
>
> "How vast the mercy and the love
>     Which laid our sins on Thee;
>   And led Thee to a cruel death
>     To set Thy people free!
>
> "But now the bonds of death are burst,
>     The ransom has been paid;
>   And Thou art on Thy Father's throne,
>     In glorious robes arrayed.
>
> "O Christ! be Thou our present joy,
>     Our future great Reward!

> Our only glory may it be
> To glory in the Lord!"

It may be interesting to some readers to see it in Jacqueline Pascal's French version:

"Jésus, digue rançon de l'homme racheté,
    Amour de notre cœur et désir de notre âme,
Seul Créateur de tout, Dieu dans l'éternité,
    Homme à la fin des temps naissant d'une femme.

"Quel excès de clémence a su ta surmonter,
    Que, portant les péchés de son peuple rebelle,
Tu souffris une mort horrible à reconter,
    Pour garantir les tiens de la mort éternelle?

"Que la même bonté t'oblige maintenant,
    A surmonter les maux dont ton peuple est coupable;
Remplis ses justes vœux en les lui pardonnant,
    Et qu'il jouisse'en paix de tu vue ineffable.

"Sois notre unique joie, O Jésus; notre Roi,
    Qui seras pour toujours notre unique salaire;
Que toute notre gloire à jamais soit on toi,
    Dans le jour éternel où ta splendeur éclaire!"

"The good father thought this so fine," continues Madame Perier, "that he urged her to proceed, but her scruples were aroused by the reflection that she had undertaken the work without due consultation."

She wrote to Port Royal to ask advice, and received an answer, Sainte-Beuve says from Agnes, Cousin says from Angélique, and where such doctors disagree we would not undertake to settle the point.

At any rate, the letter probably expresses the opinions of both sisters on the subject, and they had fortified their own by that of M. Singlin. "I have obtained M. Singlin's opinion on the questions you ask," the letter runs. "To the first" (which seems to have been an inquiry into the propriety of some employment), "he says that nuns must not work for vanity, and it would be better for you to work on it a little at a time by way of occupation. As to the second, it is better for you to hide your talents of that nature, instead of making them known. God will not require an account of them, and *they must be buried*, for the lot of women is humility and silence."

Again, "I am glad that you have yourself anticipated this decision. *You ought to hate your genius,* and all the other traits in your character which, perhaps, cause the world to retain you, for where it has sown it would fain gather the harvest. Our Saviour will do the same in His own good time. He will call for the fruit of that divine seed which He has set in your heart, and which, with patience, will become abundantly multiplied. This is all He now asks of us."

"When Jacqueline received this letter," says her sister, "she showed it to me, and, without giving any reason, begged the good father to excuse her from proceeding farther." This was, then, with one notable exception, Jacqueline Pascal's last poetic effort.

The third noteworthy production of her pen during these years was a series of fifty-one "pensées edifiantes" on the mystery of the death of our Lord Jesus Christ.

It was the custom at Port Royal to decide by lot every month on a motto, or subject of meditation, for each member of the sisterhood. The Mère Agnes often included Jacqueline in this drawing of lots, and in May, 1651, she sent her the subject given above with this kind little note: "I have drawn for you the Mystery of Jesus Christ's Death, and the same subject has also fallen to my lot. I have thereby been led to think that . . . . none of those holy desires, emotions, and actions which God inspires in us can reach their full perfection, nor aid us in the attainment of Christian holiness, until our self-will is entirely dead and happily swallowed up in God's will. When this is done, we can not fail of experiencing that resurrection which gives eternal life. Let us therefore try, my dear sister, to realize that it is the privilege of our heavenly calling to die daily, and let us not shrink from crucifying our own inclinations, if we may thereby honor Him whose death has procured for us eternal life."

These reflections of Jacqueline Pascal's on the death of Christ would be rather heavy reading, to say nothing of writing, for most young ladies of the present day, however religiously inclined. We are to notice

that they are *thoughts*—not *feelings*—and that each
one has a practical bearing.   If any girl will make the
experiment of writing out fifty-one distinct thoughts
on any one single fact, she will get an impression of
the quality of Jacqueline Pascal's mind.

We give a few extracts, choosing them on the principle of brevity chiefly:


### III.

Jesus died *in reality*, and not figuratively, or in desire only.

This teaches me that I ought to die to the world
effectively, and not to be content with imaginations
and beautiful speculations about it.


### IV.

The death of Jesus has nothing extraordinary about
it; that is to say, His body was deprived of life, as
all other bodies are, and death took possession of Him
in the posture and in the manner natural to that
condition.

This teaches me that although I ought to destroy
within me the flesh and all its desires, there should
nevertheless be nothing extraordinary nor singular in
my actions; but I should do simply those things
which are suitable to my present condition.

### VIII.

Jesus did not wait to die of old age, but anticipated death in the strength of His youth.

This teaches me not to wait till the decadence of my life before dying to the world, but to anticipate the actual by the mystic death.

### X.

Jesus died on the cross, raised above all the world, having everything under His feet, even His blessed mother.

I learn from this that my heart should be above all the things of this world, and that by this elevation of spirit, which is not proud, but heavenly, I should regard as beneath me everything, even that which is most grand and most amiable.

### XV.

Jesus died publicly, before the eyes of all who chose to gaze.

I learn from this that although my condition may expose me to the eyes of the world, nevertheless I should die to it.

### XXVIII.

I see Jesus dead in three different places: on the cross in view of the whole world; descended from the cross in the midst of His friends; and in the tomb in entire solitude; and in these three places He is equally dead.

This teaches me that in whatever state I may find myself, in conversation or in solitude, I should equally be dead to the world.

### XXX.

Jesus was clothed after His death with the garments suitable to the dead.

I learn from this to show by my dress that I am dead to the world.

### XXXII.

Even the cloth in which the body of Jesus was wrapped did not belong to Him.

I learn from this not to be attached to the things which are about me, even those which are most useful.

### XLVII.

Jesus did not enter triumphant into heaven as soon as He died to the earth, but He waited patiently several days.

This teaches me to suffer in patience the privation of celestial consolations.

### XLVIII.

Jesus died, but in dying He did not leave His own comfortless. He sent to them His Holy Spirit, which is His Divine Love, to dwell with them (though invisible), even to the end of the world.

I learn from this that in whatever manner I may be separated from my own, I ought, nevertheless, always to dwell with them by an affection which is born of God, and always assist them with my prayers.

### L.

It was by the death of the natural body of Jesus that He gave life to His mystical body, which is the Church.

This teaches me that my death to the world should be the principle of my life in God.

# THE LORD OPENS THE WAY.

# XIII.

## THE LORD OPENS THE WAY.

THUS the months and the years had passed away till September, 1651. "At that time," says Madame Perier, "my father was seized with the illness of which he died, and my sister devoted herself to attendance upon him by day and night, with the utmost zeal and assiduity. She may be said to have done nothing else, for when her presence was not needed in his room, she withdrew to her own apartment, where, as she herself told me, she prostrated herself and prayed for him incessantly with tears. But God, notwithstanding, did according to His own will, and my father died, September 24th. We were at once informed of it (being then at Clermont), but my state of health prevented us from reaching Paris before the last of November." This was the time when, as we may remember, Madame Perier "preferred to incur the expense and trouble" of taking her little girls with her rather than run the risk of possible ribbons and laces bestowed by their indulgent grandmother.

While Blaise and Jacqueline waited together these few weeks in the house of mourning, there seems to have been a renewal of the old, beautiful, tender intimacy between them.

" My brother was much comforted in his deep affliction by her society," says Madame Perier. And, doubtless, Jacqueline was as much comforted by her brother. Notwithstanding the opposition of her opinion to that of her father, her love for him was deep and her mourning most sincere. Touched by a common sorrow, the hearts of brother and sister crept naturally close together. Once more Jacqueline becomes her brother's scribe, and they write together a long, beautiful letter of mingled grief and consolation to their sister.

" Let us view death," they say, " in Jesus Christ, and not without Him. . . . . In Christ all things are pleasant, and work together for our good. Death is no exception. Christ suffered and died that He might sanctify death and sorrow.

" It is not right for us to be without grief, even as the angels who are unconscious of sorrow. Neither ought we to refuse comfort, as do the heathen in their ignorance of grace. . . . . It is our duty to let the comforts of grace overcome natural sorrow, and to say with the apostle, ' Being afflicted, we give thanks.'

"A holy man once told me that one of the most advantageous ways of showing our love for departed friends is to do as they would advise us, were they still living, to follow their counsels, and to endeavor to attain that state of holiness in which they would delight to see us."

And then Blaise cries out in his own name (though the handwriting throughout the letter is Jacqueline's), "His loss is greater to me than to the others. Had I lost him six years ago I had been ruined, and though my need of him is not quite so absolute at the present time, it seems as if he were necessary to me for the next ten years, and his presence would have been useful through my whole life."

Undoubtedly, during the three years just past, father and son had been much thrown upon each other for companionship, and the separation was the more keenly felt on that account. Perhaps, also, there was another reason for his feeling the need of a father's restraining and inspiring presence.

As we have seen, his path and Jacqueline's have been all this time diverging. Not only was he not ready to follow her up to her cold, calm heights, but his feet had, actually, for a time, turned in another (and in Jacqueline's austere judgment), an opposite direction.

That he had not lost his faith is abundantly proved by the letter from which we have quoted.

But cut off from all study, either secular or religious; deprived of the old home enjoyments by the absence of one sister and the still greater inaccessibility of the present one ; denied, both by ill-health and by his easy circumstances, the invigorating effect of manual labor, it would have been a marvel if the young man's life had not acquired a taint of *aimlessness.* At first, when the physicians had ordered him to " abandon every sort of mental occupation, and seek, as much as he could, opportunities of amusing himself," he was very reluctant to take their advice, " *because* " (keen, clear, honest logician that he was !) " *he saw its danger.*"

" At length, however, he yielded, thinking it his duty to do all he could to restore his health, and believing that trivial amusements could not harm him." And so, to use the severe expression of Jansenism, Pascal had " set himself on the world."

Margaret Perier, his niece, relieves the picture by a few slight details:

" In consequence of my uncle's miserable state of health," she says, " the physicians had to interdict all mental effort ; but a disposition so lively and energetic as his could not long remain idle. When he was no longer busied in scientific pursuits, or in religious studies requiring close application, he felt the need of amusement, and this drove him into company where he played cards and joined in other diversions. At first he did so in moderation ; but by degrees his taste for society increased, and though his life was never in the least vicious or irregular, it gradually became gay, frivolous, and useless. . . . . At length he made up his mind to follow the common routine, purchase some office, and marry."

And this is the worst that, in all the Port Royal and the family annals, can be found set down against those few deeply-regretted years.

But now his father's death recalls Blaise Pascal from whatever worldly pleasures he may have been enjoying, and the loss of that father's affectionate presence throws him back upon his sisters for the love he so much needs both to give and to receive.

How beautifully the strong, natural affection blazes up at this opportunity—that affection so soon to be resolutely smothered, though never extinguished! "May God continue in my heart," he says, "that love for you and my sister which seems to me greater at this moment than it ever was before. I feel as if the love we used to lavish on my father *ought not to be lost, but to be gathered up and concentrated on each other.* The legacy of love he left us should be invested in a deeper fraternal affection, if that were possible."

With such feelings in his heart, with Jacqueline by his side, writing for him and ministering to him in her old sisterly way, it is not strange that he should have been "much comforted," nor that he should have "imagined that kindness would induce her to stay with him at least a year, to help him in recovering from this great calamity."

But Jacqueline's purpose was exactly what it had been for three years. The Lord had now removed the only obstacle in the way of her fulfilling it. There was, then, in her view, but one thing for her to do. She would take the portion of goods that fell to her and go to Port Royal. Till her sister could come, and the property could be divided, she would stay with her brother. And while she stayed she would be his loving, sympathizing, and tender sister. She would not add to his grief if it were possible to help it. She would make the wrench as gentle as possible. "She concealed her intentions till we arrived," says her sister. "She then told me that she meant to take the veil as soon as the estate was divided, and that she should spare my brother's feelings by letting him suppose she was only going to make a retreat at Port Royal."

A month passed after Madame Perier's arrival at Paris before the estate was settled. During this time Jacqueline "disposed of everything" in preparation for retirement from the world. On the last day of December the division of property was made, and the last papers signed. Jacqueline had a part of her own share transferred to her brother, but she kept a considerable sum—her dowry for her "divine betrothal"—about which more hereafter.

Three days after the settlement she left her home forever. This is her sister's simple story:

"On the evening before, she begged me to say something to my brother, that he might not be taken by surprise. I did so, with all the precaution I could; but though I hinted something about 'a retreat,' he did not fail to be deeply moved. He withdrew very sad to his own chamber, without seeing my sister, who was then in a small cabinet where she was accustomed to retire for prayer. She did not come out till my brother had left, *as she feared his look would go to her heart.*

"I told her for him what words of tenderness he had spoken, and after that we both retired. Though I consented with all my heart to what my sister was doing, because I thought it was for her highest good, the greatness of her resolution astonished and occupied my mind so much that I could not sleep all night.

"At seven o'clock the next morning, when I saw that my sister was not up, I concluded that she was no longer sleeping, and feared she might be ill. Accordingly, I went to her bed, where I found her still fast asleep. The noise I made awoke her; she asked me what time it was. I told her; and having inquired how she was and if she had slept well, she said she was very well and had slept excellently.

"So she rose, dressed, and went away, doing this, as

everything else, with a tranquillity and equanimity inconceivable.

"*We said no adieu for fear of breaking down.* I only turned aside when I saw her ready to go.

"In this manner she quitted the world on the 4th of January, 1652, being then exactly twenty-six years and three months old."

Thus ends Madame Perier's sketch of the sister's life, from which we have quoted so often.

How touching in their simplicity are these last words! How full of suppressed, unselfish love!

"What a picture," says Principal Tulloch, "does this extract give us of this remarkable family!—the elder sister's wakeful anxiety—the younger's calm determination — the brother's half-suppressed yet deeply-moved tenderness-- the proud and sensitive reserve of all the three!"

To our mind, the elder sister, acting as medium between Blaise and Jacqueline, who dared not trust themselves to meet — quite forgetting herself in tender concern for each of them — shielding and soothing the wounded brother, yet rising to full sympathy with Jacqueline in her high resolve—always unselfish, always "*la fidèle*," forms the noblest figure of the group. Yet there is dignity in the silent Blaise, sitting "very sad," but unremonstrating, uncomplaining in his chamber. And there is a wonderful calm brightness about the noble girl sleeping "excellently" on the eve of so great and solemn a change. Was this from want of love and tenderness? Gilberte knew better than that! "*She feared his look would go to her heart.*" "We said no adieu *for fear of breaking down.*"

Port Royal opened joyous gates to the dear sister who had so long waited for admittance. Jacqueline was assigned at first to the Paris house, and entered at once upon the active duties of the convent as postulant or candidate.

It was, undoubtedly, a pleasant and a healthful change from the life of solitude and introversion she had been leading. At the same time there were inconveniences and hardships attendant on convent life which might have severely shocked the delicate, high-bred girl had she not wisely made some preparation for them. The abbesses Angélique and Agnes allowed no luxuries to themselves or to their nuns, except the luxury of charity. The utmost poverty and bareness prevailed throughout the whole building, and the nuns' cells—the only thing in the world which they could call their own—were no exception to the rule. The story is told of one of the Arnaulds, that, on going to her cell for the first time, at night, she covered the one bare little table with a white cloth and made such few simple preparations for her toilet as circumstances admitted. The abbess—her own sister Angélique—noticed it in her nightly round, and "laughed in her heart." However, she said nothing that night, but the next day the simple little appointments —cloth and all—were removed. When the young sister came to her cell the second night and found it bare again, she thought there had been some mistake and again spread a clean white handkerchief over the table. But once more it was removed, and so it went on till she had thoroughly learned the lesson and cheerfully submitted to it. It was a part of the great lesson of " the mystery of the poverty of Christ."

Jacqueline Pascal had been humbly trying to learn that lesson in her own cheerless chamber at home, and probably she found little difficulty in suiting herself to a new lack of comforts. Her dress, too—the ugly and harassing combination described by Gilberte—must have been willingly exchanged for the novice's costume—a "loose, gray robe, cut on the cross, fastened round the throat and hanging to the feet." The beauty of this dress, according to Angélique, was that "all kinds of work could be done in it," and all kinds of work were done by candidates, novices, and sisters of all degrees, from cleaning the hen-house and scouring the saucepans to the most exquisite darning and the reverent care of the altar furniture.

"We used to go into the kitchen by turns for a week together," says Anne Arnauld. "We liked hard work of all kinds, and I was particularly fond of sweeping the floors, remembering that St. Theresa took great pleasure in it. In the summer mornings we used to go into the garden and dig in silence with great zeal. We rose at two to say matins and did not go to bed again after that time. In winter the church was very cold, but no one complained of it, and our clothing was not much warmer in winter than it was in summer."

The "Constitutions of Port Royal," drawn up by the Mère Agnes, give us a similar view of humility and activity. "The novices," says this authority, "are not to be fed with milk and honey, by being humored and treated gently, but with the strong meat of self-denial and humiliations. . . . . Industry is a positive duty, each sister being expected to perform a certain amount of work daily, the more humiliating the better, and to love her task, because the Saviour stooped to practice a lowly trade, and so did His apostles. They make their own habits and shoes, as well as linen, wafers, and wax candles. Book-binding is also one of our occupations, and we make lanterns, candlesticks, and other useful articles of tin." . . . . (Embroideries and artificial flowers were never introduced at Port Royal). "When at work, the sisters are to be silent and meditative. . . . . Strict silence is enjoined for some hours of each day, except in case of absolute necessity, and even then the use of signs is recommended. . . . . Those possessing good voices are carefully trained to sing in the choir, under the direction of a leader, who must strain every nerve to prevent the possibility of a mistake or failure in the worship of the sanctuary; yet the leader is not to assume undue authority, or *permit her voice to be heard above the others!*"

One of the sweetest duties of the convent to Jacqueline was, doubtless, what was called "the perpetual adoration of the Holy Sacrament." This expression is a little startling to Protestant ears, but it only signified "that every nun was to spend a portion of each day in silent prayer before the altar, and to wait there till relieved by one of her companions." They had no set form of prayer for the occasion, but were to invoke the special aid of the Holy Spirit to bring their wishes into accordance with God's will, "*and not dwelling on their own personal wants or sins,* were to *forget self,*" and plead earnestly for the good of the Church universal and the extension of Christ s kingdom. They were taught to hope that by thus trying to imitate the blessed ones who "rest not day nor night" in their worship, and "expelling as far as possible all earthly interests from the heart, Christ would fill it with the precious balm of His grace, and perfume their poor prayers with the incense of His own merits. The remembrance of this hallowed hour was also to accompany them through the rest of the day. Their motto was to be, 'I sleep, but my heart worketh,' meaning that no occupation ought to distract their minds from continued prayer and communion with Jesus."

Of course, in addition to this daily worship in the church, and fixed hours for each one in her own cell, the sisterhood observed the ordinary Church routine of fasts and festivals. The Bible was, moreover, daily read aloud—not a common custom in a convent at that time, if it is at present. The nuns were urged to learn portions of it by heart. "Let them try to fill the treasury of their minds with God's word," say the Constitutions. "It is more desirable than gold or precious stones."

One hour of every day was allowed the sisters "in which to make confession of losses, accidents, or slight failures in duty." There was another "hour of conference," in summer, spent in the garden, where each one was permitted to speak freely, "provided she did so with discretion and grave politeness, as well as care not to interrupt others, or put herself unduly forward."

Such was the daily course of Jacqueline Pascal's life during these first months at Port Royal. We are obliged to learn of it from the convent rules and not from herself, for at first she wrote very little, even to her faithful Gilberte. Indeed, the "Constitutions" require that letters should be rarely written. They were never sent without inspection, nor were they

ever to be very affectionate. "The best way of ex-
pressing love is in prayer for its object."

Without doubt, Jacqueline was happy. But one
great burden lay on her heart—one great longing
took possession of her soul. It was the longing for
her brother's full sympathy. As the time drew near
for her to take the veil the burden weighed heavier,
the longing grew more intense. Her few letters at
this time are grave and repressed. It is not till later,
when actual trial and persecution are staring her in
the face, but when her heart is lightened of this great
weight, that we catch once more an occasional gleam
of her youthful playfulness.

# FRESH TRIALS.

FRESH TRIALS.

## XIV.

FRESH TRIALS.

THE usual period of probation at Port Royal
was a year, but Jacqueline had in effect
been on probation before she entered the
convent, and, in her case, the time was shortened to
four months.

It was arranged that she should take the veil as a
novice in May. And looking forward to that joyful
occasion, there is but one thing lacking to render her
happiness complete.

Early in March she wrote a long letter to her
brother—a letter as remarkable as the one she wrote
her father when begging for a "retreat" at Port
Royal.

"This letter reveals," says Cousin, "both the
woman and the saint, the mingled passion and ob-
stinacy which distinguish the whole family, and withal
a charming sweetness—a blending of humble entreat-
ies with the accent of command." She signs herself

already "sœur de Sainte-Euphémie," the "new
name" which she is to receive on the day of the
coming ceremony. (Strange that while cutting themselves away from all natural relationships, and breaking the most sacred bonds, these monks and nuns
must yet borrow the names of human ties to express
their ideal of their place in God's world! Father—
mother—brother—sister—they can find no more sacred titles by which to show what they believe to be
the highest and holiest estate for man or woman!)

Through the greater part of this letter Jacqueline
addresses her brother with the grave and formal
"you," but now and then she forgets herself and re-
lapses into the old familiar "thou." She begs him
by all their former intimacy to give her "his kindly
greeting" in this solemn act, and yet she reminds
him that she is now her own mistress, and can do as
she pleases without his consent! In short, the whole
eight pages are just as illogical, just as affectionate,
just as proud, as noble, and as thoroughly feminine
as was that long letter to her father three years before.

See how skillfully she touches upon every motive
which can possibly have weight in her brother's
mind:

"Do you remember the time," she says, "when I
loved the world, and when my knowledge and love of
God increased my guilt, because my heart was so un-

equally divided between two masters? Do you remember that it was *you* who first tried to convince me
that I could not unite two things so opposed as the
spirit of religion and the spirit of the world?"

"You ought, in some measure, to judge of my affection by your own, and to consider that, even if I *am*
strong enough to persevere, despite your resistance, I
may not be able to bear up against the grief it will
cause me." As if she would say, "I *am* human still,
though you may not believe it; I *have* a heart and you
can make it ache."

"You have the power of troubling my peace," she
goes on, "but you can not restore it if, through your
fault, I should once lose it. Do not take that away
which you can not give."

"Do not hinder those who do well; and do well
yourself; at least, if you have not the strength to follow me, do not hold me back."

"How strange that you should have such scruples!
You would not try to prevent my marrying a prince,
nor think, if I did so, it were not my duty to follow
him, even to a place very far removed from you."

"I await this proof of your affection," she concludes (his presence at the ceremony). . . . "Of course
my invitation is a mere form, for *I do not imagine you
would dream of staying away!* . . . . I have written
to my sister. I ask you to console her, if necessary,
and to encourage her. I tell her that if she wishes to

come, it will delight me to see her, but that if she comes in the hope of making me change my mind, her pains will be thrown away. I say the same to you. Now, do with a good grace what you must do any way; I mean, do it in a spirit of kindness, and do not make me unhappy. Farewell, my very dear brother."

This letter brought Blaise at once to his sister's side. He came the day after receiving it, and saw her for the first time, perhaps, since she left him, in the convent parlor through the grated window.

"He was nearly wild with a terrible headache," Jacqueline writes to Madame Perier—"the result of my letter. Yet he was much softened; for instead of the two years' delay he had asked before, he only wanted me to wait till All Saints' Day"—the last of October. "But seeing me determined not to put it off long, and yet complaisant enough to allow him a little more time to get accustomed to the thought, he gave up entirely, and even expressed pity for me that I had been obliged to delay so long that which I had set my heart upon. Nevertheless, he did not return at the appointed hour to settle the exact time, but M. d'Andilly, by my request, was good enough to send for him Saturday, and to argue with him so skillfully and yet cordially that he agreed to everything we wished."

Thus far Jacqueline had gained her point, but painful difficulties were yet to come—difficulties of a kind quite unthought of by her. She had no idea of entering Port Royal empty-handed, and took it as a matter of course that her portion of her father's property was to go to endow the convent. But to her great surprise, her brother and her sister—yes, even her faithful Gilberte—were not inclined to agree with her in this view. If she had chosen the spiritual riches, they seemed to think it but right and natural that they should have the earthly. They viewed the case, as poor Jacqueline says, "in an entirely secular manner." The mixture of grief, vexation, and mortification in her heart at this unexpected *contretemps* is curious to witness. For the proud and high-spirited daughter of M. Pascal to come to Port Royal portion-less, is, indeed, a bitter thing. But she humbles herself even to this, and "begs earnestly" for admission as a "lay-sister." "If my reception must be a gratuitous one, I thought that out of gratitude to the sisterhood, for the double favor of welcoming me without a dowry, I could do no less than serve them as a menial for the rest of my life. . . . . But God, the Searcher of hearts, knew me to be unworthy of an office so honorable in His sight, and that my past and present pride needed a punishment instead of a reward. He therefore restrained Father Singlin from giving his consent."

In a "Relation," which takes up fifty pages of

Cousin's volume, Jacqueline gives the details of this whole affair. The paper was written not in her own interest, but as part of the "Memoirs of Port Royal," and notwithstanding its length, it is worthy the reading of any one who is interested in the study of character. It shows that the infirmities of human nature, in convents and out of them, were much the same in the seventeenth century as now. Yet at the same time it shows how far love and right feeling and religion can go toward conquering those infirmities.

At first Jacqueline has nothing but indignation and a fine scorn to bestow on her brother and sister. Her years of mortification had not placed her beyond the possibility of genuine anger and vexation. "My resolution," she says, "which they thought so unkind, gave my friends a fine chance of moralizing over the instability of human affections!"

. Both Blaise and Gilberte wrote, giving as reasons for their refusal, the entaglement of her share of the property with their own, and various technical difficulties. *If she would wait four years*, till all claims on the estate had been settled, they would think of it. "Disingenuous arguments!" she exclaims, "which, had they been less irritated, they would never have named! Not that these reasons were actually untrue," she goes on to say, "but *they were not such as we had been accustomed to use with one another!* Just think, my dear mother, how these letters made me feel!—

written in a style so changed! . . . . my grief became so violent that it seems wonderful I lived through it."

"This strong expression," says Sainte-Beuve, "is no exaggeration. She *does* nearly die of it. Her intense, enthusiastic nature, frustrated on the point of the triumphant fulfillment of her vow, and that, too, by a thrust from those whom she loves, *is* almost overpowered. And we recognize here the same tender, conscientious, womanly heart that a few years later falls a victim to its own scruples and reproaches."

The dear Mother Agnes sees Jacqueline's heavy grief and sends for her—her "fille chérie"—for a long private talk. With the greatest tact and wisdom she deals with the wounded heart. "Only eternal things are worth such emotion as this," she says. "Temporal matters ought never to call forth these tears—only the *real* evils, sins, deserve those." And then, trying the effect of a little gayety, she declares that she is "really astonished! that it is almost incredible that *she, a novice—a novice of Port Royal!*—ready to make her profession—is capable of being afflicted by *anything*, least of all by such a *bagatelle* as a little money!"

But though the novice's heart is lightened for a time, Agnes sees that she has not effected a cure. So, in the kindness of her heart, she sets out for *Des Champs* to tell Angélique all about it, and Father Singlin, too, who happens to be there for a few days

The Mère Angélique's advice is characteristic. "Tell her to relinquish it all to her relatives, and not to mix herself up in the matter any further. And let her give her whole mind to her approaching profession."

Dowry or no dowry, lay-sister or lady-boarder—the profession was the main thing in Angélique's mind. That was a matter of course. When was Port Royal—since *she* had anything to do with it, certainly—known to delay a profession on the score of poverty?

But good Father Singlin has the guidance not only of Jacqueline's conscience, but of the Reverend Mother's as well, and by this time he has gained a good deal of facility in reading souls. "He did not entirely agree with our Mother," says the *Relation*, "for he feared there might be too much generosity and too little humility in the advice!"

And he "improved" the occasion (perhaps on the way back to Paris, whither they both returned the next day), by a few short remarks. "When we have overcome the avarice of wealth," he said, "we ought to beware of falling into the opposite extreme and becoming greedy of praise, and ostentatious of our generosity, while we despise those who still cling to their property."

After some further conference, however, he advised Jacqueline to adopt the Mère Angélique's plan, but he chose to dictate her letter to her brother himself, "lest my own words should be too warm," says Jacqueline, frankly. "This letter," she continues, "could not be short, and it kept me busy till evening so that I did not see our Mother. But, on the next day, as was her custom after returning from the country, she sent for all the novices, and when my turn came to salute her, I could not help saying that I was the only sorrowful one among the sisters, who were all delighted at her return. 'What?' said she, 'is it possible, my daughter, that you are still sad? Were you not prepared for trials?' . . . . And then she talked to me a long time *on the emptiness of all human affection, keeping her arm around me with much tenderness!'*—dear, inconsistent Angélique!

"The next day, also, 'having noticed that my looks were unusually sad,' she left the choir before Mass began, and sending for me, did her best to give me comfort. Not content with this brief effort of kindness, as soon as Mass was over, she signed to me to follow her, and then supported my head on her bosom for a full hour, caressing me all the time with a mother's tenderness. I can truly say that she omitted nothing in her power that could charm away my distress."

"I told her," says Jacqueline, naïvely, "that it was the injustice done to the establishment that troubled me, and that personally I was neither hurt nor angry, but simply indifferent. 'You are mistaken, my daughter,' said she. ' Nothing is more painful or hard to bear than wounded affection. I know you feel deeply the injustice done to the House, but your own share in this gives you a keener pang, for self-love mingles in everything we do, and is the mainspring of this mighty sorrow ! '

" She was then so good as to give me the details of several similar cases, without mentioning names. I suppose this was done as much for the sake of affording me that species of comfort derivable from companionship in misery, as to convince me that we never take the interests of justice so much to heart as when they concern ourselves."

" Now forget all that is past," says the good Mother, at the end of this long talk, " and speak and write to your friends as if nothing had occurred, merely telling them that you confirm your resignation (of the property) in their favor. *And you must do this in all sincerity*, avoiding a spirit of pride, as if you had been more generous than they, and avoiding, also, a wish to coax them into obliging you. If our actions do not arise from genuine love they are worthless."

Pascal, it seems, was at this time absent from the city for a few days, but when he came home and found Jacqueline's letters awaiting him, he at once presented himself again in the convent parlor. Port Royal's nobility had challenged his, and he was not found wanting ! He undertook " *à l'instant*," to manage the whole affair, and without waiting to free his sister's portion from its entanglement with the rest of the estate, to make a gift in his own name to the convent, "taking upon himself all risks and charges." Thus suddenly and simply was the difficulty removed.

As to Pascal's first position in the matter, Reuchlin explains it thus: "In the case of twins it is frequently observable that the death of one is soon followed by that of the other. Blaise Pascal and Jacqueline Pascal were twins in soul, and when the former strove to prevent his sister's complete identification with Port Royal, he was in reality struggling for the right of his own independence—fighting for his own life. Another pretext for delay presented itself in this difficulty about the property, and he eagerly seized it." But as soon as he saw that it was useless, that Jacqueline's determination remained unshaken in spite of the worst he could do, he gave up without another word. Gilberte, for her part, seems to have acted only out of sympathy for her brother, and from the natural "secular" view of the matter. But she yields in the end as gracefully as does her brother.

And so, at last, the eve of the solemn day had actually come—the day so long delayed, so ardently desired! Is Jacqueline as happy as she expected to be? A few days before, she wrote to her sister:

"There is nothing but sorrow everywhere" (referring to the war), "yet I am full of joy, for I am to take the veil on the glorious feast of Trinity. After so much opposition, it seems like a dream to find myself so near it. I shall fear that it is only an illusion till the ceremony is really over. But I will not waste time in expatiating on my happiness, for you can not doubt it." Did ever expectant bride write a happier letter on the eve of her wedding-day?

The nuns went rather early to their cells that May evening, for to-morrow was to be a great day for them. Perhaps Jacqueline Pascal lingered, like St. Agnes, a little while at her window looking at the solemn stars.

The airs from the garden were soft and sweet, and the pink horsechestnut blossoms were dropping now and then through the stillness, as they drop now on May evenings in the gardens of Paris. That "noble house" in the Faubourg St. Jacques, was very full that night, for many of the sisters had come in from Port Royal *des Champs* to see the ceremony. The next day's dinner had been prepared overnight, so that lay-sisters and all might have an opportunity to be present at the services.

But scarcely had quiet settled down on the house when voices and quick steps were heard about the gates, and the frightened women were soon out of their beds. It was war-time, and they were living in constant expectation of danger. They found, however, that it was not a troop of soldiers who had taken possession of the house. It was only a band of nuns who had been driven out of their convent at Etampes and had walked all the way to Paris.

"These poor sisters reached the Faubourg St. Jacques about nine o'clock," says the story. "Some of them had friends in the city, but knew not where to find them; others were friendless. It was quite dark, they had no guide, no guard, and did not know what to do. As they passed the gates of Port Royal one of them recognized the convent. She bade her companions be of good cheer. Madame de Port Royal" —Madame *du cœur* Royal, as she was often called— "would take them in."

They were not disappointed. It was against the rules for an abbess to receive members of another community without the permission of the archbishop. "But Angélique said, 'Charity is above law,' and opened her gates." And now was made evident the good Providence which had led them to cook to-morrow's dinner overnight! These sisters must be fed first of all. Then came the more difficult task of finding beds for them. "We began to gather up all that we could," says one of the nuns. "There was nothing to be met in the passages and on the stairs but sisters dragging their beds, pillows, coverlets, mattresses, and doing it all with the heartiest good-will."

The next day, with all these unexpected guests and with the two communities of Port Royal to witness her profession, Jacqueline Pascal took the veil as novice. We do not know whether her brother and sister were present. No details of the ceremony have been preserved. It was probably conducted according to the "Constitutions" of the convent, with great simplicity. Few guests from "the world" were permitted; all attempts to excite public interest by display were prohibited. The dress of the candidate must be plain and inexpensive. Pearls and other ornaments were forbidden; and instead of the usual entire severance of the hair, the abbess only cut off a little from the ends. "If the candidate should afterward repent of her consecration she was not to be deterred from re-entering society by the loss of that feminine adornment."

# A BUNDLE OF LETTERS WHICH TELL THEIR OWN STORY.

# XV.

### A BUNDLE OF LETTERS WHICH TELL THEIR OWN STORY.

TO M. Perier, during an alarming illness of his wife:

"*July* 31, 1653.

"MY DEAR SISTER AND BROTHER:—I write to you both, if God permit this letter to find you both in a state to read it, which, after your note of the 24th, I scarcely dare to hope. You can imagine the state of my own feelings; I do not pretend to express them. But I think it my duty in this extremity to render all the assistance I can, both to my sister and yourself. I pray for you as often as possible, and our mothers have frequently reminded the sisterhood to commend her case to God. . . . . We can not have a better opportunity of testing whether we possess real faith. . . . .

"If it please Him to grant my sister the happiness of seeing His face in preference to ourselves, why should

we oppose her blessedness?   I see no blessedness to
be found in this world except in giving up all things
for God; but even this is not to be compared with
the full possession of Him and the certainty of never
losing that felicity. . . . . .

"God knows that I love my sister more than I did
when we were both in the world, and yet it seemed
to me then that nothing could increase my affection;
but whereas at that time my chief wishes and anxieties
were for her life (which always has been, and still is,
dearer to me than my own), they now relate to her
eternal life.   Therefore, violent as my grief is, and
though I am continually in dread of hearing the fatal
news, *trembling so that I can scarcely stand if any one
looks as if he were going to speak to me,* yet, when I
take into account the misery and dangers of this present life, especially for a person immersed in worldly
occupations, I can not but accuse myself of selfishly
desiring my own benefit rather than hers.   And so
my most earnest prayers to God are that the infant
may be an heir of grace and that the mother's illness
may be sanctified. . . . . . Tell her to remember the
beautiful saying of M. de St. Cyran, that 'the sick
should look upon their bed as an altar whereon they
continually offer up the sacrifice of their life for God
to take at His pleasure'; and this other: 'The pains .
and various inconveniences of illness are sounds that
serve to warn the virgins of the Bridegroom's ap-

proach.' Let her hope to go in with Him to that blessed marriage.

"SŒUR DE SAINTE EUPHÉMIE,

"(*Religieuse Indigne*)."

Under the same date Jacqueline urges her brother-in-law, in case of her sister's recovery, to testify his gratitude by leaving his wife and family and becoming a recluse. Happily, he did not follow this advice, but we are told that, after this time, he wore a girdle lined with iron points, though his humility kept this fact a secret till after his death. He used also to have a plank in his bed, and made his bed himself in order to prevent discovery.

To Madame Perier, bearing joyful tidings:

"*Dec.* 8, 1654.

"It is not right that you should longer be ignorant of what God has wrought in the heart of one so dear to us; but I wish you to learn it from himself, in order that your every doubt may be done away. All that I now have time to tell you is that God has graciously given him a great wish to be entirely devoted to his service, though in what mode of life is not yet determined. For more than a year he has felt a thorough contempt for the world, and an almost insupportable disgust for its votaries; and yet, though his excitable temperament would naturally lead him to extremes, he behaves with a moderation that encourages me to hope for good. He has put himself entirely under Père Singlin's direction.

"Though his health is worse than it has been for a long time, it does not in the least affect his resolution, which shows that the reasons he formerly urged were only a pretense.

"I perceive in him a humility and submission, even toward myself, which astonishes me. I have now no more to add, except that it is evident another spirit than his own is at work within him. Farewell; let all this be kept secret, even from him.

"I am yours entirely,

"SISTER EUPHÉMIE."

To Madame Perier, giving further particulars of the good work:

"PORT ROYAL, *January* 25, 1655.

"MY VERY DEAR SISTER:—I wonder if your impatience to receive intelligence has been greater than mine to communicate it; yet, as I had no time to waste, I was afraid to write too soon, lest I might have to unsay what I had prematurely said. But now things are at a point where you ought to know of them, let the result be, by God's good pleasure, what it may.

"It would be doing you injustice not to relate the whole story from the beginning.

"He came to see me toward the close of last September, and during the visit, opened his heart to me in such a way that I felt a deep pity for him.  He acknowledged that in the midst of his occupations, which were numerous and of a nature to excite in him a love for the world, he still often felt a desire to leave it altogether.  That, by reason of his aversion for the follies and amusements of society, and by reason of the constant reproaches of conscience, he found himself more detached from the world than he had ever been before; but that, on the other hand, God seemed to have forsaken him, and he experienced no longings after Him. . . . .

"This confession gave me great surprise and delight, and from that time I began to hope for him as I had not done before.  If I were to recount all his other visits in detail, it would fill a volume, for they were afterward so frequent and so long that I seemed to myself to have no other work to do than to follow him and watch his progress.  I did not attempt to hurry him in the least, but I saw him growing in such a way that I scarcely knew him for the same person.  You will see it also, if God carries on the work, and particularly in his humility, submission, self-distrust, even to the point of *scorn* of self and desire to become as nothing in the esteem and memory of man.  This is what he is now; only God knows what he will become.

10*

" There were many visits and much conflict on the subject of choosing a spiritual guide. He saw the necessity of having one; but, although the person best suited to him was already found and he could not bear to think of any one else, yet his self-distrust made him afraid of being guided by partiality. *I* saw clearly enough that this hesitation only arose from the independence yet remaining in his soul, and catching at any excuse for avoiding the complete subjection to which he was tending. But I would not influence him. I merely said that I thought it was our duty to select the best physicians we could find, both for the soul and for the body. . . . . At length his mind was made up. But our task was not over yet, for M. Singlin hesitated to undertake the charge, chiefly on account of a long-continued infirmity which prevents his speaking without great pain.

" Meanwhile many things occurred, too long and unimportant to be repeated here ; the principal event being that our young convert came of his own accord to the conclusion that a temporary withdrawal from home would be serviceable to him. M. Singlin was then at Port Royal *des Champs* for the benefit of his health; and therefore Blaise (although he was terribly afraid of having it known that he held communication with the convent)'resolved to go thither under pretext that business called him into the country. By changing his name, leaving his servants in

some neighboring village, and proceeding on foot to
M. Singlin, he hoped that no one would recognize
him or discover his object, and that, in this way, he
might effect a temporary retreat.

"I advised him not to take such a step without
consulting M. Singlin; and M. Singlin, on his part,
forbade it altogether.  M. Singlin wrote him a beautiful letter, and in it he constituted *me* as my brother's
directress until God made his own duty plain. . . . .
When M. Singlin at length returned, I entreated him
to release me from my dignity, and said so much that
I obtained my desire.  They then both thought it
would be best for Blaise to make a trip into the country for the sake of being more alone than he could
be in town.  His particular friend (the Duc de
Roannez) had returned, and took up nearly all his
time.

He, accordingly, made the Duke his confidant
(receiving his consent, which was not given without
tears), and set out the day after Epiphany. . . . .
He has procured a room, or rather a cell, among the
recluses of Port Royal, and thence he writes me that
he finds himself extremely happy, being lodged and
treated like a *prince*—a prince of St. Bernard's
stamp, dwelling in a lonely spot, where the profession of poverty is carried out as far as discretion
will allow.

"He is present at every service from Prime to

Complines, and does not find the least inconvenience in rising at five o'clock.

"It seems to be God's will, also, that he shall fast as well as watch, though, in doing so, he must defy all medical rules which forbid him to do either. But he finds that his supper begins to give him pain in the chest, and I think he will omit it.

"He will not miss his directress, for M. Singlin has provided him with a confessor, M. de Saci, with whom he was not before acquainted, a man who is beyond praise, and who has completely charmed him already."

(M. de Saci was one of Madame le Maître's sons, an elegant writer, translator of the Bible, and one of the brightest lights of Port Royal).

"He told only two persons where he was going when he set out. However, it was suspected. Some say he has turned monk; others hermit; others, again, that he is at Port Royal; and he knows all this, but does not care for it. . . . . .

"I have not been able to finish this letter till to-day, Feb. 8.

"Business just now detains Blaise at home, but, as soon as he can. he will go back to his solitude. . . . . . He is anxious to do something for our little cousin, the daughter of Pascal the overseer; and as this convent is very charitable, we hoped to get her received here as a boarder. But I doubt whether either mother or child would be willing. Write me about it, please, as soon as you can and say how we had better manage it. I am very anxious she should come, for I look upon her as a sister and can not think of her situation, either bodily or spiritually, without a shudder. Besides, she is my father's niece, and I can understand how he would have felt for her from my own feelings toward your children.

" SISTER EUPHÉMIE."

To M. Pascal during his retreat at *Les Granges* (Port Royal *des Champs*):

" *January* 19, 1655.

" MY VERY DEAR BROTHER :—It gives me as much delight to find you cheerful in solitude as it used to give me pain, when I saw you immersed in the gay-eties of the world. I hardly know, however, how M. de Saci gets along with a penitent so full of happi-ness. Instead of expiating worldly pleasures by un-ceasing tears, you are only relinquishing them for more reasonable joys and a more allowable play of fancy.

" For my part, I think your penance very moderate indeed, and there are few people who would not envy you it ! "

A few more playful, but rather obscure allusions follow: " And now," says the writer, " I hereby put an end to the willful nonsense of this letter. Your

eager desire to renounce every semblance of worldly
distinction is very praiseworthy. . . . . The same must
be said of your wooden spoon and earthen platter
about which you wrote me. These are the gold and
precious stones of Christianity. None but princes
should have them on their tables. We must be truly
poor in spirit if we would deserve such an honor,
which, according to the Marquis de Renti, should be
denied to common people. My only comfort is that,
this kind of kingship not being hereditary, it may be
acquired. . . . .

" I was before you in the discovery that health de-
pends more on Jesus Christ than on the maxims of
Hippocrates. *Spiritual regimen often cures bodily ailments.* Unless, indeed, God sees fit to strengthen us
by means of sickness. Certainly it is a great privilege to have sufficient strength of body to do what
is enjoined for the cure of our souls; but it is none
the less a privilege to take chastisement from Him.
In either case we are well, if we are in Him. We
are not told, ' if any man will come after Me let him
perform works requiring great strength,' but, ' let him
deny himself.' And sometimes a sick person may do
this better than one in health."

To the same;—a fragment :

" *December* 1, 1655.

" I have been congratulated on the great fervor of
devotion which has lifted you so far above all ordi-

nary customs, that you consider a *broom* a superfluous piece of furniture. . . . . I think that, for some months at least, you should try being as clean as you now are dirty, in order that you may show that you can succeed in humble and vigilant *care* of the body (which is your servant), as well as you have succeeded in humble *négligence* of it. After that, if you again find it glorious and edifying to others to be dirty, you can do so; especially if it be a means of holiness, which I very much doubt. St. Bernard did not think it was."

To Madame Perier in answer to inquiries as to Jacqueline's promotion in the convent:

" *June* 23, 1655.

"I had thought of answering this part of your letter in the same style in which you wrote, but I can not do it. All my gayety leaves me when I approach the topic. And I therefore entreat you to believe every word of what I shall now tell you, for I am perfectly serious.

"I dare say my employment here has been represented to you as much greater than it in fact is. After all, it is a mere nothing, and I do not suppose that any one but myself would consider it of consequence.

"But it is quite a responsibility for me, who would much rather keep in the background, and am *fit for nothing but to bustle about in a tiny cell,* or *to sweep the house;* for this last is an accomplishment I have become quite expert in, as well as in washing dishes and spinning. You see I have learned to be very handy.

"The employment assigned me, then, is to remain with the novices and keep an eye on the newly-arrived candidates, in order to prevent such little mistakes as they are likely to make at first. I also look after their little external wants, and see that they are provided with shoes, stockings, pins, thread, etc. . . . . And that you may have no more cause to complain of my reserve, I will tell you that it is also my duty to advise them in regard to their behavior. Now, you know just what I have to do. . . . . My sister Madeleine is always on the spot to correct me if I do wrong. . . . . But for all that, I can not help trembling when I think that I hold the destiny, so to speak, of five or six girls in my hands, and that they are in a measure dependent on one so imperfect. . . . .

"I must acknowledge that, when you were here, I often felt that it was scarcely right to keep this a secret from you, to whom my heart has always been so open, especially when you frequently asked me what it was that kept me so busy. I had even made a memorandum to ask our Mother Agnes whether this confidence were not due you, but God permitted me always to forget it, and, since you left, it has never occurred to me. Neither have I mentioned it to my brother, and if he knows it, some one else has told him.

"There is a great advantage in having to teach others the ways of God ; . . . . but it is very difficult to speak of God in a godly manner, and *there is great danger of feeding others from our own penury instead of from His abundance.* Pray for me that my two mites may be as acceptable to Him as the large alms of the wealthier. Farewell, dear sister. Yours ever in the Lord,

"SISTER EUPHÉMIE,<br>" An unworthy nun."

To the same, in answer to inquiries as to the best method of educating her children :

"PORT ROYAL, August 15, 1655.

"MY VERY DEAR SISTER :—I take a large sheet of paper, because it is my resolution, by God's help, to send you a long letter. When I first read the one you forwarded by my brother I did not intend to answer it at all. It seemed to me that I was very far from having the requisite ability for such a task, and, besides that, I ought not to undertake it. For there is nothing, in my opinion, so provoking as to see a little novice, whose eyes have scarcely begun to dis-cern the true light, taking it upon herself to enlighten others, and to become their torch-bearer. It is really unendurable !

"But since, on account of the humility of our mothers and the illness of Père Singlin, I am totally unable elsewhere to procure the aid you are seeking, I do not know that there is any harm in saying to you what I have said to myself, *for I feel as if you and I had but one heart and one soul in Christ Jesus.*

"When I had written thus far, it occurred to me that M. de Rebours (one of the confessors) might, perhaps, be able to give some advice. I broke off, therefore, in order to consult him, and now write what he says : * * * *

"To M. Pascal, making inquiries in regard to his new method of teaching children to read :

"'October 26, 1655.

"'Obedience and charity lead me to break silence before you do, my very dear brother, and when I least expected it ; I tell you this, lest you should be scandalized at my writing.' (She alludes, probably, to some mutual vow of silence for a certain time).

"'Our mothers have commanded me to ask all the particulars of your method of learning to read without learning the names of the letters. I can see very well how a child can be taught to pronounce some words in that way, but how do you manage with silent consonants following a vowel?—for instance, such a word as *en*? . . . . I see difficulties in the system, but then, I am sure, you have also foreseen them and provided for them.

"'So much for obedience; now for the charity.' (She then begs a favor of him in behalf of a poor young girl of their acquaintance.) 'I will not apologize for giving you the trouble. Charity is its own recompense.

"'Did you think of me on the 10th? That is the day of my baptism, you know. Remember me also to-day. The 26th of every month is dear to me since God gave me grace on that day to cast off forever the habiliments of the world. May you and all who belong to you be ever the Lord's. I belong to you not less by grace than by nature. Properly, indeed, I consider myself your daughter; I shall never forget it.'

"SISTER EUPHÉMIE,

"*An unworthy nun.*"

The system of teaching here spoken of was introduced by Pascal into the Port Royal schools, and through their text-books, adopted afterward throughout France. It is now used in many English schools, and has been introduced somewhat in the United States. Cousin says: "A method of orthography certainly adds little to the glory of the great mathematician, the great scientist, and the great rhetorician, yet it serves to bring into relief that exactness and clearness—the special attribute of Pascal's genius—which he carried into the smallest as well as into the greatest things."

Pascal's system of logic, set forth in his little treatise, " De l'art de Persuader," was about this time also adopted at Port Royal.

# TEACHING THE CONVENT SCHOOL.

# XVI.

## TEACHING THE CONVENT SCHOOL.

THE letters we have just read tell us better than any other words could do, the story of Jacqueline Pascal's life between 1652 and 1655. They show us the increasing honor in which she is held by that household of noble women among whom she has found her home. They show the great confidence reposed in her by her superiors, evidenced by her appointment as Sub-Mistress of the Novices before she had herself passed her novitiate. And still stronger proof of confidence and high esteem is the fact that careful, conscientious Abbé Singlin placed in her hands the infinitely momentous and delicate task of guiding her brother's newly-stirred conscience.

They very touchingly show that brother's trust in her as he makes visit after visit and unburdens his troubled heart before her; and they show her elder sister's exaggerated reverence when she asks of the inexperienced novice how she shall best bring up her family.

But, above all, these letters give us a hint of the inner life—a glimpse at that "secret greenness" which "only One" can fully see.

We perceive a rapid growth of character. We see a great increase of sweetness—of love and of joy—in her heart. The *beauty* of holiness is beginning to be apparent. Instead of the chilling virtues of those first years of devotion to God there is a pleasant warmth and light. She is not afraid now to tell her brother and sister how much she loves them. "It seems to me we are but one heart and one soul in Jesus Christ," she writes to Gilberte. "Did you think of me on the 10th?" she asks Blaise, showing how completely the old freedom and sympathy is established between them and how sweet it is to her.

In every way, indeed, there is an increasing naturalness and healthfulness in her religion, as there must be in all spiritual life, the nearer it approaches to Him who *is* the Life.

Not that faults are wanting. As long as we know Jacqueline Pascal we shall see those, yet more and more, from this time, they seem to be the faults of her century, her education, her Church, rather than faults of character.

Undoubtedly, Jacqueline's great joy in her brother's conversion hastened her spiritual growth. Joy is good for souls. Whatever may be said and may be true of the blessed effects of sorrow, those who have had great sorrows and great joys know that joy is the natural atmosphere of the soul. He who has swung open the doors of heaven to His children knows this well.

And so, when the desire of this sweet woman's heart is granted, when her cup runs over—we see her coming back to the naturalness and freedom of her early days. Her heart comes again as the heart of a little child. She does from joyful enthusiasm, not from forcing duty, what her hand finds to do.

It was a great year for the Port Royalists—this year of Pascal's definite identification with them and farewell to the world. In their histories it forms a distinct era, and other events are dated from it, as one dates from the accession of a sovereign.

In the family annals the change is known as his "second conversion." Many striking and minute accounts of it are given. We will content ourselves with Jacqueline's story as we have read it in that long letter to their sister. It can not fail to be a faithful picture, though less sharp in its outlines than most of the Jansenist writers have made it.

There can be no doubt that, during those years when mental activity was denied him, Blaise Pascal made a thorough trial of material pleasures, yet the straitest of the Jansenists—those who most bitterly

11

deplore those years of defection—are careful to say that no hint of vice ever attached to his life. "His feet, indeed, trod the mire," says one, "but his divine wings remained forever unsoiled."

During these years, a young nobleman—the Duc de Roannez—was Pascal's most intimate friend. There is a suspicion of an attachment on Pascal's part for the duke's sister, a girl of sixteen—an unspoken love, however, if it existed at all, and hopeless, probably, in the lover's mind, on account of the great difference in rank and fortune.

A treatise on "Love," probably written about this time, goes toward establishing the theory. But students of Pascal's life differ in their opinions, and it is one of those questions which can never be settled. Sainte-Beuve believes that "Pascal never passionately loved any being but his Lord and Saviour."

Mdlle. de Roannez became for a time a novice at Port Royal, but was urged by her friends into a marriage which proved most unfortunate. Pascal corresponded with her at intervals throughout his life. Her brother, the duke, became warmly interested in the Port Royal party, and was one of the editors of the first edition of Pascal's "Thoughts."

When such a young man as we know Blaise Pascal to be "came and sold all that he had" and followed Jesus, we should expect great ardor and enthusiasm from him, and we find it showing itself

sometimes in painful forms. Even the nun Jacqueline, as we see, is obliged to reprove him for
his neglect of the body, while he revels in his new-
found spiritual joy. Ill-health, doubtless, deepened
the naturally somewhat ascetic tone of Pascal's
mind, and we see through all the remainder of his
life a relentless crushing out of much that is beautiful
and noble in human nature.

He was a most ingenious self-tormentor and did not
always remember that those who loved him were, of
necessity, included in the torment. While Jacqueline's
character is budding anew into fragrance and bloom,
his seems to be growing hard and dry, like some
brown lily-bulb which gives no hint of the glory and
sweetness within. Both bud and bulb will burst into
spotless beauty when the full summer comes!

But at his harshest and his driest, Jacqueline, his
twin soul, understands him.

"I felt astonished and discouraged by his coldness
and occasional rebuffs," writes Madame Perier, speaking of a time when he was ill at her house. "I did
not then know that he thought it wrong to testify
affection. I wrote about it to my sister and complained that my brother was unkind and did not love
me, and that I really seemed to displease him even
when I rendered him the most affectionate services.
My sister wrote me that I was mistaken, that she
knew the contrary. He loved me dearly,—as well as

I could desire,—and if opportunity offered for him to help me in any way, he would prove by deeds what he thought it wrong to express in words. And, indeed, I afterward found it so."

We have mentioned her brother's conversion as one reason for Jacqueline's happiness. Another reason was her busy life. " I am never able to write above two dozen lines," she says, "often not more than five or six without being interrupted by some question." For, in addition to her other duties, Jacqueline was soon appointed to teach in the convent school of Port Royal de Paris. It was a large and popular boarding and day-school—as popular, probably, as any young ladies' school in Paris is to-day. Mrs. Schimmelpenninck says, " It would be easy to cite a prodigious number of young ladies educated in these schools " (that at Port Royal *des Champs* and the one in the city), " who have since edified the world, the court, or the cloister by their wisdom, piety, and talent. It is well known with what sentiments of admiration, gratitude, and reverence they always spoke of the education they received at Port Royal."

Anne Arnauld had been for some years the Principal of the Paris school. The pupils were very fond of her, especially the younger ones. No wonder! for we are told: "It was so pleasant to her to gratify them that she could not help giving them sweet meats." However, being a nun—a Jansenist—a conscientious and truly loving as well as an indulgent woman—"she always prayed before giving them that the children might not like them very much!"

"One day," the story goes, "the children were naughty, and Sister Anne left the school-room saying she should not return, for it grieved her too much to see how little love they had either for God or for their duty." The children, on their part, spent the morning in tears, "entreating the other teachers to go and fetch Sister Anne and tell her how sorry they were. At length some one went, and she relented immediately and came to them. They flocked around her, and she said it was a great consolation to her that they were sorry for their faults, because God forgave those who repented, and it was, therefore, quite right that she should forgive them also. With this, she drew a bag full of sugar-plums from under her mantle and distributed them, saying that when St. Louis wept as he thought of the Passion of our Lord he found the tears which fell upon his lips were sweet as honey; and she gave them the sugar-plums in order that they might remember that when we weep for our faults our tears are sweet."

Sometimes Sister Anne would bear the burden of the children's faults and do penance for them herself, for she could not pass over the sins, nor could she bear to punish the children. "She had not learned," says Frances Martin, "that the tenderness of their

Father in heaven was as great as her own, and thought that she must appease Him by her own sufferings."

And now to this delightful Sister Anne and to one or two others of the talented Arnauld sisters, is added Jacqueline Pascal with her clear, well-trained intellect, her talent, her noble, womanly character.

Fortunate school-girls! Justly do the "Mémoires" say: "The education they here received under the sisters of Pascal and of Arnauld, was far different from that elsewhere afforded to ladies."

The new teacher was never so demonstrative as Anne Arnauld. She proved her love in a very different and certainly a far less beautiful manner.

In the opinions of her superiors she was clearly a successful teacher, for, after two or three years' experience, she was directed by Father Singlin to draw up a code of "Règlements pour les Enfants," according to the Port Royal plan. This was added to the "Constitutions," though with the caution that in other places it might not be easy or even advisable to carry them out fully. Some children might not be able to endure so strict a discipline, neither could all teachers enforce it, without losing the love and confidence of their charge, "which is all-important."

No one who loves children can read these rules without shivering. "Yet," says Vinet, "where must be the eyes of those who can read them and not dis-

cover them to be full of the most considerate tenderness?"

And we must remember that the chilliness and
harshness which so offends us is not to be charged to
the writer so much as to the whole of the false, unnatural system of which she was one of the few re-
deeming features.

These poor little Port Royal girls are to rise at
half-past four or five, according to their size and
strength. "They must rise promptly, not allowing
themselves time to get thoroughly awake, for fear of
yielding to idleness."

Prayer, both silent and audible, is the first duty,
and then the elder ones comb each other's hair " in
perfect silence." This "deep, morning silence," is
strongly insisted on and lasts, so far as we can see,
through the greater part of the day. For, after
Prime, at half-past six, the beds are made by the
girls in couples, still in silence. Next, hands are
washed and mouths rinsed with wine and water,
and breakfast follows, during which " one of them
reads the Martyrology for the day."

At half-past seven, all withdraw to the work-room,
" where they must diligently improve their time and
keep a strict silence. If it is necessary to speak they
must do so softly, so as not to interrupt those who
are old enough to hold communion with God. Even
the little ones are taught not to speak, though they

are allowed to play when their work has been well
and silently done, but each must play by herself so
that there may be no noise." And here is the first
glimpse of the tenderness of which Vinet speaks, as
the writer adds, in her own simple, kindly way, " I
have found that this solitude does not trouble the
children, for when they are used to it, they seem
to amuse themselves very merrily." We have a
second view of her tenderness, and, at the same time,
a specimen of shrewdness and good management in
this remark: "We teach them that they ought to
perform disagreeable tasks with more industry and
good nature than pleasant ones. But, nevertheless,
*we do really humor them in their tasks* as far as we
can, *without allowing them to perceive it.*"

At eight o'clock, the governess reads till half-past
eight, when all go to church.

Then comes a writing lesson (silent), before which
each offers a short prayer that God would help her
to perform that duty aright. "We try to impress
their minds gently with a holy habit of never beginning an action of any importance without prayer."

At eleven, they all examine themselves and afterward repeat the *Confiteor.*

At length, "the dinner bell rings." Can they be
girls now and run down, waiting with bright faces
around the table till their teacher joins them? "On
entering the dining-hall, they curtsey in pairs and do

the same in passing any of the sisters. They stand modestly in their places till grace is said, their sleeves falling over their hands. . . . . They must keep their eyes always down, not looking on either hand, but quietly listening to what is read."

On leaving the dining-hall, they have a recess. And now for a little natural life!

"The little ones are kept apart from the elder ones in order that the latter may converse more quietly and discreetly." "If the recess is held in a room, the elder ones gather in a circle round the mistress and talk modestly and sociably, according to their ability." "They may be allowed to play at innocent games, such as battledore and shuttlecock. Not that our girls avail themselves of this permission, for all of them, except the very youngest, are so fond of work that, as I have said, a holiday is irksome to them." "The children are to avoid every kind of personal familiarity, and *never to caress, to kiss,* or *even touch one another* on any pretext. *Neither must the elder ones pet the little children.*

"The recess closes with prayers asking for grace to enable them to pass holily the remainder of the day."

It would be wearisome to follow these school-girls through the whole day, till the evening bell calls them from their walk in the garden to undress " with silence and dispatch," and go each to her separate bed. We will simply make a few more extracts from the rules :
12*

“We avoid talking much to the children, feeling that instruction does more good if they are not wearied with it.”

“We do not seek to render them too spiritually-minded, unless God himself has made them so, because either they might set too close a watch upon themselves and so weary the mind and fancy, instead of communing with God, or, on the other hand, might feel too much discouraged at finding it impossible to attain the perfection demanded of them.”

“I find it a good way of forming a habit of industry to allow them to do at recess some work which they like and can not do at any other time. I taught them, for instance, to make worsted gloves, and as they can only do this during their recess, they are very eager after it.”

“We are careful to make them speak politely, hold themselves uprightly and gracefully, and curtsey when they enter or leave the room.”

“They must not speak of the singing of the sister-hood, remarking that one sister sings better than another, etc.”

“Uncharitable conversation is specially prohibited, and they are taught never to say anything that might be unpleasant to one of their number, though in itself harmless, because it is enough to know that any one present would prefer some other topic of discourse.”

"We try to make them yield precedence to one an-other from that holy politeness which charity alone produces.

"I think that really to do children any good we ought never to speak or act for their benefit without first looking to God and asking His holy aid."

"We ought to be very kind and tender toward them, never neglecting either their internal or external wants, and showing them that we grudge nothing to serve them."

"Example is the most effective method of teaching. For the devil helps them to remember our slightest failures, and hinders them from remembering the little good we do."

"As to their trivial defects, I think it best seldom to notice these, because they otherwise gradually get accustomed to be found fault with."

"They ought to be treated politely, spoken to with respect, and yielded to where it is possible."

"We ought to consider them as sacred deposits placed by God in our hands, for which we must render an account to Him. Therefore it is best to say little to the children, and much to God on their behalf."

More and more, as we proceed, does the hidden love and wisdom become manifest, and as we read the final word we are ready to say with Mrs. Schimmel-penninck, "although many treatises on education have appeared in modern times, and many which have been distinguished for the splendid talents of the writers, perhaps not many among them surpass in true wisdom, in a deep knowledge of the human heart, or reality of experience, these ' Règlements' of Jacqueline Pascal."  " Nor is it to be forgotten, that whilst the press teems with numberless theories, this little, but inestimable work details a system which was tried, and that with unexampled success, for above sixty years; and which, at the end of a hundred and fifty years, still entitles its author to the reverence due to transcendent piety and the admiration due to super-eminent talent."

# THE MASTERPIECE AND THE MIRACLE.

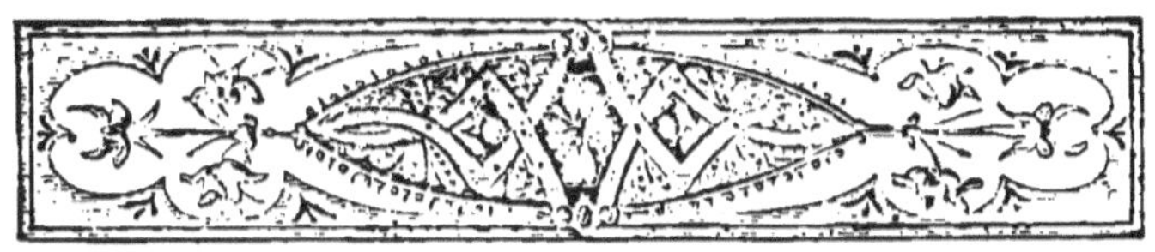

# XVII.

## THE MASTERPIECE AND THE MIRACLE.

ST. CYRAN and Jansen were both in their graves, but the truth they loved lived after them. Its enemies, too, were active still. The hatred of the Jesuits was the rightful inheritance of the second generation of Port Royalists who are now on the stage.

In order to understand that hatred and the climax it now reached, it will be well at this point to recall some facts in regard to both Jesuits and Jansenists.

In the first place the Jesuits had an old grudge against the father of the Arnaulds, on account of a remarkably forcible and eloquent charge he had made against them when he was a rising young advocate. This success, Pascal wittily said, was the "original sin" of Jansenism. And some of the later sins had been of the same sort. Such were those flourishing and popular schools and the widely-circulated school-books. And such were the increasing numbers of talented and influential men and women constantly joining the Port Royal ranks. We remember, too, that there was an old quarrel with Pascal in the matter of his atmospherical experiments. Father Nöel and his confrères could not be expected to love the Jansenists any better after Pascal became one of their number.

More than this, the strict morals and ascetic habits of these people were a constant though silent reproach of the lax principles and "casuistic morality" of Jesuitism. The ideal of true Christian living was plainly more nearly approached at Port Royal than in the Jesuit colleges.

"A little church born of the Spirit, within the visible and regnant church," the Jansenist body has been fitly called. Disowned, indeed, they were by the Romish communion, but "they obstinately refused to accept that disavowal." It was "grievous" to them, as Pascal said, "to find themselves in a strait betwixt God and the Pope." But they did their best for many years to stand in that difficult and dangerous position.

We must remember, now, in addition to all this, that the Jesuits had great influence with the Government. "They especially coveted," we are told, "to guide the consciences of men in power." "There were very few princes on the throne, nobles in the realm, dignitaries in the Church, or religious houses belonging to any order, which were not, either directly or remotely, under their influence." The young king, whatever else had been lacking in his education, had been well indoctrinated by his Jesuit confessor, Father Annat, with hatred of the Jansenists. And it was an easy matter to persuade Anne of Austria and Cardinal Mazarin that the Port Royal schools were "hot-beds of heresy" and must be abolished.

Early in 1656, the year to which Jacqueline Pascal's letters have brought us, the matter seemed to have reached its crisis. Over the heads of the Port Royalists hung the censure of the Sorbonne (the University of France) on a book of Arnauld's, "De la fréquente Communion," and, worse than that, the author's condemnation by the Pope. And after bewildering and almost interminable disputations, lasting from July of one year to May of the next, the Holy See had condemned the celebrated "Five Propositions."

These propositions were referred to in the chapter on Jansen, but we must look at them more closely here. They were five statements, which Father Cornet, a Jesuist priest, had with marvelous subtlety and art framed out of Jansen's "Augustinus." "They were worded,' Mrs. Schimmelpenninck tells us, "with the most artful ambiguity. The phrases were so contrived as to be capable of two constructions, widely differing from each other." In some cases it was only the question of a comma's position in the sentence.

Now, there was not one of these propositions which the Jansenists would not have condemned, if bearing the meaning the Jesuits imputed to them. But they denied that they were to be found in any such sense in the "Augustinus."

Hence, when a "formulary" was drawn up for them to sign, condemning these propositions, they signed without any ado, but, one and all, added a line stating that the propositions were not to be found in Jansen's book, and pointing out wherein they differed.

This was disappointing. Simple, straightforward truth had cut the twisted knot! But the Jesuits were equal to the emergency, as we shall see.

They began their work of vengeance by getting an order from Government for the breaking up of the Port Royal schools—the schools for boys. "The officers of the police, accompanied by a troop of archers, were sent to Port Royal *des Champs*, where they made a list of the schools. They then proceeded to each, and immediately turned out all the masters and scholars." Racine, the poet, was a pupil in one of the schools at the time of the dispersion, and has given an account of it in his "Histoire de Port Royal." The recluses were also driven away from *Les Granges* on pain of imprisonment. Pascal took lodgings in Paris, where he soon had plenty of work to do for his cause.

"Immediately after, an order of council was signed

against the nuns. It was resolved that every scholar, postulant, and novice should be turned out of both houses of Port Royal." The decree had been given and was on the point of execution when two remarkable events occurred which had the effect of delaying the persecution for five years. One of these events was the publication of Pascal's most famous work, the "Provincial Letters"; the other was a so-called miracle, effecting a wonderful cure on the person of Margaret Perier, Jacqueline's niece, who was a novice of Port Royal.

The story of the "Provincial Letters" is an interesting one:

There was a good old nobleman, the Duc de Liancourt, living in Paris, who went one day to his church in the parish of St. Sulpice to confess. The duke had once made a retreat at *Les Granges* and he had a little granddaughter in the boarding-school at Port Royal.

When he had finished his confession that day the priest said, "I can not give you absolution. You are guilty of two sins which you have not confessed : you have a relative who is a *pensionnaire* at Port Royal and you have dealings with those heretics—the gentlemen recluses of *Les Granges*."

The aged duke admitted the facts, but was not willing to confess them as sins, and quietly went away without absolution. But the affair made a great deal of talk.

Arnauld ("the great Arnauld," Angélique's young-est brother,) had been trying to keep still after his last condemnation.   But he was a born controversialist and he could hold his peace no longer.

He came out in a series of letters on the subject, and that was the signal for a wordy tournament, two months long, between himself single-handed and the doctors of the Sorbonne.   Arnauld produced ream after ream of solid argument (in Latin), and was written down or talked down by the Jesuits, with Père Annat, Louis Fourteenth's confessor, prominent among them.

The Duc de Liancourt and his affair were very soon left behind, as the combatants rushed once more into the labyrinth of the " Five Propositions."   Eighteen or twenty sessions of the theological faculty were spent on the question *"du fait"*—that is, whether the propositions *were, in fact, in* the " Augustinus " ; the remainder of the time on the question *du droit*— that is, whether the propositions were orthodox if they *were* there.

On the 14th of January—a few days before the dis-persion of the recluses—Arnauld was censured on the question of *fact*, and the doctors went on to take up the question of *right*, with the prospect of another censure on that.

The great leader returned to his friends at Port Royal, we may well believe a little dispirited.   "The gentlemen there," Sainte-Beuve tells us, " all begged him to write something in his defense—something addressed to the *public*." His "labored, geometric apologies," in Latin, addressed to the Sorbonne, did not come anywhere near the people, and they, seeing all this array of ecclesiastical and scholarly authority against him, could only suppose that the very foundations of the faith were in danger. "Address yourself to the public," urged his friends. "It is time the people should be undeceived. Are you going to let yourself be condemned like a child that has nothing to say for itself?"

"He wrote, therefore," says Margaret Perier in her Memoirs, "and read his production to them all. But no one gave it any praise. M. Arnauld understood their silence, and as he did not covet applause, he said, 'I see very clearly you think this a poor performance, and you are right,' and turning to M. Pascal, he added: 'You—you are young,—you might do something.'"

"M. Pascal wrote the first Provincial, and read it to them. M. Arnauld cried, 'That is excellent; every one will like that; it must be printed.'"

"This was done," adds Pascal's niece simply. "The success it had is well known, and the work went on."

"The success it had,"—it and its seventeen successors—was immense. Perhaps no literary success was ever more immediate—and probably no series of eighteen letters ever more completely reversed the public sentiment of a nation. Jansenism and Jesuitism, as they had been known in these interminable theological debates, for so many years, were matters of indifference to a large proportion of the population. But these letters!—everybody wanted to read them. The court ladies laughed over their satires. The keen, clear-headed French middle classes enjoyed their sharp, unerring truthfulness. Thinking people were convinced by their arguments. Unthinking people were carried away by their eloquence. "By his inimitable pleasantry, Pascal succeeded in making even the dullest matters of scholastic theology and Jesuitical casuistry as attractive to the people as a comedy; and, by his little volume, did more to render this formidable Society the contempt of Europe than was ever done by all its other enemies put together."*

"They killed the Jesuits," says Sainte-Beuve. "I say *killed* deliberately. I know the Jesuits still live, and, in some respects, prosper. But I maintain that they are slain in the sense that they are forever fallen from the center of action which they occupied, and have lost the access to the government of the world." "It was a shaft from a bow doubly strung," says an-

---

* Henry Rogers, author of "The Eclipse of Faith."

other writer,*—"strung with genius and piety, and his enemies could not recover."

The Chancellor of the Jesuit College was so enraged at the effect of the letters that his physicians ordered him to be bled seven times. And far off in the provinces ecclesiastical councils which had met to censure Arnauld changed their minds and censured the Jesuits instead.

Margaret Perier gives us a glimpse of her uncle's life while he was writing these immortal letters:

"He went to an inn, where he was not known, and remained there at work under the name of M. de Mons." (The old home at Clermont and the *Puy du Dôme* were not forgotten). "M. Perier, his brother-in-law, took lodgings in the same inn as a stranger from the country, not letting the relationship be known."

One day they were very near discovery. Father Defretal, a Jesuit, a friend and relative of M. Perier's, called on the latter to give him a friendly warning. "He said that the Society of Jesuits were firmly persuaded that M. Pascal, his brother-in-law, was the author of those 'little letters' which were having such a run in Paris, and that M. Perier would do well to warn him and advise him to stop writing them or he might find himself in trouble."

---

* Essay in the *North British Review.*

After a long call, " the Jesuit went away, repeating that M. Pascal ought to be warned and to beware. M. Perier was greatly relieved at his departure, foi at that very moment there were spread out upon his bed to dry a score of copies of the seventh or eighth letter. A Jesuit brother, who had accompanied Father Defretal, sat very near the bed, but luckily the curtains were drawn and the papers were not discovered. M. Perier at once ran up-stairs to tell M Pascal, whose room was overhead, though the Jesuits had no idea of his being so near them."

Neither had the Jesuits any idea where these letters were printed, though they tried hard to find out, for, with equal boldness and sagacity, Pascal had them printed under the very shadow of the Jesuit college.

Some of the Port Royal gentlemen, who, though scattered, were in frequent communication, had doubts as to the propriety of using these carnal weapons of wit and satire in defense of the truth. Good Abbé Singlin, in particular, thought that " merriment was out of place when applied to religious subjects."

As for Pascal himself, ascetic and sufferer that he was, it was probable the sure instinct of genius rather than any personal delight in mirth that led n'm to unsheathe this shining blade. "When we regard his life, so afflicted, sad, and short," says Villemain, "we can scarcely understand that superabundance of humor with which this man floods the arid fields of scholasticism." Yet we can not help thinking that he must have thoroughly and heartily enjoyed himself for once, as he gave free play to all those varied powers he had been trying so long to cramp and kill.

He defends himself for the use of satire and for his entire mode of attack, in this passage of the sixteenth letter:

"I was asked if I repented having written 'Les Provinciales.' I reply that, far from having repented, if I had to write them now, I would write even more strongly. I was asked why I have given the names of the authors from whom I have taken all the abominable propositions I have cited. I answer, that if I lived in a city where there were a dozen fountains, and if I certainly knew that one of them was poisoned, I should be obliged to warn everybody to draw no water from that fountain; and, as they might think it pure imagination on my part, I should be obliged to name him who had poisoned it, rather than expose all the city to the danger of being poisoned by it. I was asked why I had employed a pleasant, jocose, and diverting style. I reply that if I had written in a dogmatical style, it would have been only the learned who would have read, and they would have had no necessity to do it, being, at least, as well acquainted with the subject as myself: thus, I thought it a duty to write so as to be comprehended

12

by women and men of the world, that they might know the danger of those maxims and propositions which were then universally propagated, and of which they allowed themselves to be so easily persuaded.

"I was asked, lastly, if I had myself read all the books I have cited. I answer, No; for in that case it would have been necessary to have passed my life in reading very bad books; but I have read through the whole of ' Escobar '* twice, and, for the others, I caused them to be read by my friends. But I have never used a single passage without having myself read it in the book cited, or without having examined the subject on which it is adduced, or without having read both what precedes and what follows it, in order that I might not run the risk of quoting what was, in fact, an objection to a reply to it, which would have been censurable and unjust."

One of the strongest proofs of the genius of these letters is the fact that, notwithstanding the difference in time, in country, in belief, in habits of thought, they are interesting reading to us to-day.

*M. Louis de Montalte*, the supposed writer (again we have a hint of Clermont in the *nom de plume*), is an honest provincial gentleman, of much ignorance and great *naïveté*, who sets out for Paris to gain information in regard to the theological disputes of the age, and particularly the doctrines of the Jesuits.

---

* A celebrated Spanish Jesuit authority.

He addresses himself to a worthy Jesuit father, who, in his boundless admiration for his own order, and in the hope of gaining a convert, details without hesitation — indeed, with triumph — all the arts of casuistry.

"The arch simplicity with which the provincial involves the worthy father in the most perplexing dilemmas—the expressions of unsophisticated astonishment which but prompt his stolid guide eagerly to make good every assertion by a proper array of authorities—a device which, as Pascal has used it, converts what would have been in other hands only a dull catalogue of citations, into a source of perpetual amusement—the droll consequences which, with infinite affectation of simplicity, he draws from the Jesuit's doctrines—the logical exigencies into which the latter is thrown in the attempt to obviate them,—all these things, managed as only Pascal could have managed them, render the book as entertaining as any novel. The form of letters enables him at the same time to intersperse the most eloquent and glowing invectives against the doctrines he exposes."*

This book of Pascal's is an acknowledged French classic. Voltaire declared it to be the first work of genius in French prose. Before Pascal the language had been heavy, involved, Latinized. Pascal "threw

---

* Henry Rogers, author of " Eclipse of Faith."

off the yoke" of Latinism, "and formed the clear, exact French." "As Corneille is the father and founder of French poetry, so is Pascal of French prose," says Cousin. And Voltaire again remarks that "Molière does not excel these letters in wit, nor Bossuet in sublimity."

A wonderful transparency is the chief characteristic of Pascal's style. "We see," says Faugère, "Thought herself arrayed in her own chaste nudity like an antique statue."

His wit is as delicate as it is keen. "Probably no one ever knew so well when to stay his hand."*

"The remarkable simplicity which characterizes Pascal's style is owing to the great labor he bestowed on his writings."† Nicole says that he often spent twenty days on a single letter, and some of them were written seven times over before they satisfied him. "This letter is a very long one," he once apologizes, "simply because I had not time to make it shorter."

The second remarkable event which delayed the persecution was the wonderful cure ascribed to the agency of the Holy Thorn.

Margaret Perier, from whose "Memoirs" of her uncle and aunt we have more than once quoted, was at this time a child of ten years, a member of the

* Rogers.          † Villemain.

school of Port Royal de Paris. She had been afflicted for three years and a half with what was supposed to be *fistula lachrymalis* of the left eye. The bones of the nose were said to be diseased, and the whole case was a most malignant one, distressing even to read about. The physicians had made up their minds to cautery as a last resort, and M. Perier, who had been absent in Auvergne for a time, was hastening back to be present at the operation.

Jacqueline tells the story of the cure in a letter to Madame Perier, dated March 29, 1656:

"Last Friday, M. de la Potherie" (an assiduous collector of relics) "sent hither a very handsome reliquary to our Mothers, having within it a splinter from the sacred crown of thorns, set in a little sun of gilded silver, in order that the whole community might enjoy the sight. Before returning it, they had it placed on a little altar in the choir, and when an anthem had been chanted in its honor, each sister went up and kissed it on her knees, and so did the children, one by one.

"Sister Flavie, their governess, made a sign to Margaret as she drew near, to touch her eye with the relic, and herself took it up and laid it on the spot, hardly thinking what she was doing. When all had retired, it was sent back to M. de la Potherie.

"That same evening, Sister Flavie, who had forgotten the circumstance, heard Margaret say to one of the little girls, ' My eye is cured ; it does not pain me at all now.'  Not a little surprised, she went to the child, and found that the swelling in the corner of her eye, which in the morning was as thick as her finger-tip, and very long and hard, had quite gone down, and the eye itself appeared as healthy as the other, and looked precisely like it."

The sisterhood proceeded with their usual calmness and good sense in the matter.  Mother Agnes (Angélique was at *des Champs*) was informed at once, and the next day she told Jacqueline Pascal.

They then waited a week, saying nothing about it, and at the end of that time Jacqueline wrote to the child's mother: " It really needs far more faith for any one who did not see her in her former state to believe that the eye was diseased than it does for those who did see her to believe the cure was produced by a miracle."

The doctor came to see her now, and the child was brought to him without a word being said.  He began to press, and probe, and examine.  " Don't you remember what a bad eye I had?" said the little girl.

" That is just what I am trying to find," said the doctor, "but I see no traces of it."

Thereupon Sister Flavie told him what had happened.  He asked if the cure was instantaneous. The child confirmed her statement that it was, upon which he said he was willing to declare upon oath that such a cure could not have taken place without a miracle.

Waiting two weeks longer, seven physicians and surgeons examined the case and made a report to the same effect.

M. Perier, in his great joy, spoke freely about the matter, and all Paris was soon ringing with the story. Anne of Austria was at first skeptical, but after sending M. Felix, the king's first surgeon, to make an examination, she was obliged to accept the universal verdict. Then the Grand Vicar of the Archbishop of Paris inquires, approves, and verifies, and the miracle is publicly sanctioned by the Church.

The Provincial letters had convinced one class of minds. The miracle convinced another class. Port Royal all at once became fashionable again. The church was so crowded at the weekly Friday services that seats had to be secured months beforehand. The ladies of the court begged the privilege of making retreats at both convents. There were almost daily conversions to Jansenism. The Queen of Poland, the Princess Guemenée, the Marquis de Sevigné, and a long list of dukes and duchesses were among those who frequently sought retirement in the cloisters, and, according to Mrs. Schimmelpenninck, "edified the world by an upright and godly conversation."

The most remarkable conversion was that of the Duchesse de Longueville, sister of the great Condé.

She seems to have become, indeed, a changed woman, and the same is true of her brother and sister, the Prince and Princess of Conti. "Their houses, retinue, and equipage became marked with strict economy. Their princely revenues were poured into the bosom of those whose fortune had been injured by the late civil war. They did not refuse to make the most humiliating and public acknowledgments of their guilt. Nor did they ever afterward spend more than was absolutely necessary on themselves; till, after a lapse of many years, all the provinces injured by the war had been fully indemnified by their princely donations."

It is quite beyond the scope of this little book to discuss the miracle of the "Holy Thorn." Indeed, we think with Sir James Stephen that "time must be at some discount with any one who should employ it in adjusting the balance of improbabilities" in this case.

We know that, as Sainte-Beuve says, "it would have been impossible for either Blaise or Jacqueline Pascal to lend themselves to anything like deception," and it is evident from their letters that they were both humble believers in the miracle.

Neither could any of the Arnaulds have been parties to the deception, if deception there were. It was much against Angélique's taste to have the matter talked about, and she said that if she had prayed for a miracle she should have asked that one might be performed upon the soul rather than upon the body.

After this great event, the bann of silence was removed from Jacqueline Pascal's muse, and by order of her superiors, she wrote a long poem in honor of the miracle. Cousin tries to find in it some echo of Corneille, but we are inclined to agree with Sainte-Beuve in thinking it "parfaitement détestable." In the awakening of nobler powers that little gift of versifying had been lost.

12*

# SORROWFUL DAYS

# XVIII.

## SORROWFUL DAYS.

IT is pleasant to think of the next three or four years—years of peace and plenty—when the nuns returned to their unmolested worship, when the recluses gathered again at their beloved farmhouse, and this whole little community of the Lord's faithful ones rejoiced in what seemed to them His visible smile and blessing.

These were busy years for Jacqueline. She was promoted to the post of Sub-Prioress of Port Royal *des Champs*, and left Paris never to return. Her letters are few and brief, but cheerful. Whatever her attainments in self-mortification, it is impossible that she should not have felt a noble pleasure in her brother's great success. The nuns were not allowed secular reading, but, for once, they had access to the choicest that French literature could give them, in these " Provincial letters." Jacqueline refers to them once or twice, always in that tone of unsurprised and assured calm which is so beautiful to see in the "sisters of genius." The world, to be sure, may be going mad over this remarkable performance, but they?—they are not astonished—they have known all the time that their hearts' beloved could do this thing!

Whatever complacency the author himself may have felt in his work so splendidly done, he was careful to check it at once, as he did every feeling of pleasure. Madame Perier tells us: "He wore an iron girdle lined with points, next his naked flesh, and whenever there came to him any feeling of satisfaction in having assisted or advised another, or when he took pleasure in the place where he was, or in any circumstance whatever, he gave himself a blow with his elbow, to redouble the violence of the constant pain and make him remember his duty. This practice appeared to him so useful that he continued it through his increasing feebleness till the close of his life. . . . . His great maxim was to renounce all pleasure and all superfluity, and he *labored without ceasing* for mortification."

In February, 1660, Jacqueline writes a letter to her nieces, Margaret and Jacqueline Perier, who are both now at Port Royal *de Paris*. This is the only specimen of her handwriting now extant—a "beautiful handwriting and orthography," Cousin tells us.

"My very dear nieces," she begins, "you have so much reason to complain of me that I can not find any excuse for myself. It will, therefore, be a shorter way to ask the forgiveness which I doubt not you will grant; for if I were to bring forward some excuse that is not exactly true I should both injure myself and set you a very bad example. . . . . I can assure you, my dear sisters, it seems to me as if I could forget myself ere I forget you, and the less I testify my love, the more I feel it."

We may judge of the busy life of the Sub-Prioress by this letter to her brother, of November, 1660:

"Good-morning, and a happy New Year to you, my dearest brother. You will not doubt my having wished you this most cordially when the year began, though I could not tell you so till its close. I dare say you wonder at my mentioning it at all, but it is right you should know that my complete dedication of this year to God has not robbed you of anything you had reason to expect from me, for I have prayed for you continually. Oh, when I think how peacefully this season of separation, which we naturally expected would prove so painful, has passed away, and how swiftly this year has fled, time seems of such small importance that I can not help longing for eternity. But I am not going on with so extensive a train of thought, which, indeed, I began unintentionally." . . . . After various salutations to friends, she concludes: "To yourself I say nothing; you can judge of my love by your own, and you know that I am entirely yours in Him who has united us more closely in the bonds of grace than in those of nature."

Early in the year 1661, troubles once more thickened about Port Royal.

Mazarin died, and what little influence Anne of Austria had, died with him. Louis XIV. had "placed his conscience in the hands of the Jesuits," and they, at once, saw their opportunity and seized it. The "Five Propositions" were once more marshalled out, —"those celebrated propositions which *are in* the 'Augustinus' but nobody has ever seen," as Pascal said, and which, according to another gentleman who read the whole book carefully through to find them, "were there *incognito* if they were there at all." A "New Formulary" was drawn up, running (in part) as follows:

"I condemn, from my heart and with my mouth, the doctrine of the five propositions of Cornelius Jansenius, *which are contained* in the book entitled 'Augustinus,' which both Pope Innocent X. and Pope Alexander VII. have condemned."

Not only ecclesiastics, but all the nuns and school-masters were required, under very severe penalties, to sign this paper. No exception was made in favor of those who had never seen the "Augustinus" or who could not read Latin!

It was, of course, impossible for the Port Royalists to sign such a paper.

" Persecution," says Tregelles, "now began in earnest. The dungeons of the Bastile were crowded with those who refused to violate their consciences by subscribing what they did not believe. The very passages of the prison were occupied with prisoners.

" M. de Saci, the nephew of the Mère Angélique, carried on during his imprisonment his well-known version of the Holy Scriptures. Henri Arnauld, Bishop of Anjou, and three other bishops, refused to accept the formulary, let the consequences be what they might. But it was upon Port Royal itself that the principal fury of the tempest discharged itself."

In April, 1661, there came an order that all the pupils in the two convents should be sent back to their homes within three days. And the spring and summer following are crowded full of sorrow.

The Mère Angélique was now old and suffering from the disease of which she soon died. But the day before that fixed upon for the dispersion, she said good-bye forever to her beloved valley of Chevreuse, and was carried on a litter to the Paris house.

" On her arrival she found the street thronged by an immense concourse of people, the gates of the convent closely guarded by sentinels, and the courts full of armed police; she was carried into the house between files of archers. She found the whole community in tears and lamentations." There were thirty-three boarders in the Paris house, not including,

of course, the novices, candidates, and nuns. Many
of these young pupils were orphans, and knew no
other home than the convent, and when the time
came for them to go, their sobs and cries resounded
through the house. It was equally hard for the nuns
to know that they were to see these children no more,
" for they were tenderly attached to them."

"The mournful scene was prolonged eight days,
for some of the parents lived in the country and could
not reach Paris sooner." The children would throw
themselves in a crowd upon the nun who had charge
of them, "weeping and holding fast by her dress."
Some of them entreated to be received at once as
novices that they might stay, and others begged to
be made lay-sisters, as the servants were not ordered
away. But in a few days there came another order
to expel every candidate and novice. Many touching
and thrilling scenes are given us in the "Mémoires."

Angélique and Agnes were true mothers to their
whole flock in these days of trial. They inspired,
comforted, advised, wept and prayed with their children, as it is given to mothers to do at such times.
Agnes wrote a very beautiful letter to the King in
regard to certain novices, whose cases we need not
detail here. "The king praised the letter," we are
told, but paid no heed to its humble request.

Angélique, from her bed of death, also wrote an
appeal to Anne of Austria. But all was useless. In

the course of a few days seventy-five young girls were removed from Port Royal de Paris, and nearly as many about the same time left the other house. Jacqueline's two nieces, the Periers, were sent home to their mother, who was then living in Paris. Their aunt wrote to them in June—a letter full of consolation and of warning. She advises them to retire as much as possible from society. "I do not mean you to be discourteous," she explains, "nor to seclude yourselves entirely, but to seek retirement when not actually obliged to mingle with society, and when you are to *snatch a few moments frequently for lifting your hearts to God.*"

The scholars, novices, and candidates were gone from both houses. The large, plain rooms were empty and desolate, and the busy Sub-Prioress, doubtless, had time now to sit down quietly to write and think. And now comes the Grand Vicar of the Archbishop of Paris, to go through both convents and question each nun in turn as to her belief. Jacqueline's account of her own examination is published in the "History of the Persecutions of the Port Royalist Nuns." She is very modest and humble—a true daughter of the Church—yet we catch an inkling now and then of the same quick wit and clear reason which, in her brother's brain, involved the worthy Father of the "Letters" in so many "logical exigencies."

"I am not accustomed to dive into matters unconnected with duty," she answers to one question, but when pressed for her opinion, she gave it simply and clearly.

At another ready answer, "he smiled a little." Once he asked her, "How comes it that so many persons are lost eternally?" "I confess to you, sir," she replies, "this thought often troubles me when I am praying, and I can not help saying sometimes, 'O my Lord! how can it be, after all Thou hast done for us, that so many souls should perish miserably?' But when these thoughts come, I repress them, not daring to pry into the secrets of God, and I find satisfaction in praying for sinners."

The Grand Vicar answered, "That is quite right, my daughter."

When he asked if she had taught the novices certain doctrines, she said: "As I avoid puzzling myself with these topics, it is not likely that I should seek to puzzle them. On the contrary, I have tried to have them as simple-minded as possible."

At the end of the conference the examiner said: "You are right, and God be praised for it. I believe you are speaking to me in all sincerity. Send me another sister."

And yet, after all these things, the nuns would not sign that little formulary. "Pure as angels and proud as devils!" exclaimed the angry archbishop. They would not sign!

How could they? How could they declare that certain things were contained in a book they never had read and never could read? They did not *believe* them to be there. They loved the truth, and "they clung desperately" and heroically to "the one shred and particle o truth they had discovered." That one particle of truth was enough to make them free—free from blind obedience to a corrupt Church, and free from fear of their adversaries.

As the Grand Vicar completed his examination at Port Royal de Paris (in July), he passed through the room where the Mère Angélique lay very near her end. "How do you feel, Reverend Mother?" asked the ecclesiastic.

"Like a person who is dying," she answered, tranquilly.

"Do you speak of death so calmly?" said he. "Does death not alarm you?"

"No," answered she. "I am incomparably more alarmed at what I now see taking place in this house." Then, rousing herself and speaking with all her old energy, she added: "Oh, sir, sir, this is man's day; but the day of the Lord is coming, and that will explain all, and avenge all!"

A few weeks later, in the midst of the storm of persecution, the good mother passed quietly to her rest. Many were her expressions of love to her dear daughters during those last days, but "Jesus—Jesus, my

Lord, my righteousness, my strength, my all!" were
the last words upon her lips.

And still the nuns would not sign! The court-
yard of the Paris house was full of mounted police
and archers, and masons and carpenters were busy
walling up the very gates of the monastery, and thus
rendering their home their prison. Père Singlin,
de Saci, and all their confessors were in concealment,
and both houses were deprived of all religious guides,
except the Jesuits. Still, they would not sign!

In this extremity some of their best friends be-
thought themselves of a compromise. A treaty with
the archbishop was opened, for the purpose of obtain-
ing a modified declaration (*mandement*), to which
these women might be willing to subscribe their
names. The scattered leaders met, with much risk
and difficulty, in Pascal's room to talk the matter
over. Some of the meetings were rather stormy.
Arnauld and Nicole were in favor of a signature of
this modified formula. Pascal was confined to his bed
with the illness from which he never rallied, but his
mind roused itself to its full strength to consider this
question which came so near him. He was in favor
of " standing by God's truth at all hazards, even if it
involved disobedience to the pope." Arnauld ably
argued the wisdom of trying to make duty to the
Church consistent with the truth, and skillfully represented the helpless condition of these nuns.

Pascal was stubborn "in his unconscious Protestantism." Duty to the Church *could not*, in this case, be made consistent with the truth. "No, no," again and again he cried, "you can never save Port Royal, but you *can* be traitors to the truth!"

At the last conference the majority of those present, yielding to Arnauld and Nicole, voted for the compromise. "Seeing which, M. Pascal, who loved truth more than anything else, and who, in spite of his weakness, had spoken with great earnestness in order to impress his convictions upon the others, was so overcome with grief that he fainted, entirely losing voice and consciousness." When he had recovered himself, and all had gone away except the Duke of Roannez and another intimate friend, "Madame Perier asked him what had occasioned the swoon. He replied, 'When I beheld so many persons to whom God has made known His truth, and who ought to be its defenders, thus giving way, I could not bear it.'"

And how was it with Jacqueline? How was that twin-soul of Blaise Pascal's settling this question?

In the quiet of Port Royal *des Champs*, beneath the solemn hills, with no knowledge of what was passing in her brother's room in Paris, she thought the problem out and came to her own conclusion. "Strange to say," says Cousin, "though not aware of the meetings at Paris, Jacqueline used the same arguments and even, in some .cases, the very same words that Pascal had done." She could not understand, any more than he, how men claiming to be the defenders of the truth, could even *seem* to abandon it on any consideration of expediency. " Brought face to face with danger, her intrepid heart broke forth in proud yet pathetic strains, reminding us of some of the finest passages of the ' Provincial Letters.' "

The advice of the leaders was formally signified to the nuns. It was that they should sign this modified document, "with a distinct exception in favor of Jansen's meaning." Not only did Arnauld urge this step, but Father Singlin, from his place of concealment, wrote them a letter advising the same. It is doubtful whether Jacqueline ever knew her brother's position in the matter.

But before she would yield, this heroic woman made one more effort. Cousin says: "We ask of all who yet retain any sympathy with energy of character and with the beauty of an unselfish love for truth, if they have ever met with many pages of greater sublimity and strength than are found in Jacqueline Pascal's ' Letter on signing the formulary '? "

This letter is worthy, in every way, of Pascal's sister. " It is an echo of his own manly and heart-stirring tone."

" I am convinced," she boldly declares, " that in

this course there is safety neither for body nor soul. Truth is the only real Liberator."

"What are we afraid of?" again she cries. "Banishment and dispersion, the seizure of property, prison, death, if you will—but are not these things our glory? Let us either give up the Gospel or carry out its principles and be happy in suffering for the truth."

Satire does not fail her. "I admire the ingenuity of the human mind, as displayed in the perfection with which the '*Mandement*' is drawn up."

"I know very well that the defense of the truth is not women's business. But perhaps when bishops have the cowardice of women, women ought to have the boldness of bishops."

And, at last, in the note to Arnauld in which she incloses the letter, the whole noble, womanly heart comes out as she concludes: "Forgive me, my dear Father, and do not imagine that though I seem courageous, nature does not dread the consequences. But I trust that grace will support me."

The Prioress of Port Royal *des Champs*, a much older woman than Jacqueline, shared the scruples of her subordinate, and did not hesitate to tell Arnauld that she did so. "And that great man," says Cousin, "instead of being irritated, did his best to answer their objections in a long letter, which unfortunately has been lost."

13

At length, a last communication from Arnauld—
Jacqueline calls it "a note of command"—was sent
to them, and, one sad day, the nuns in solemn procession signed the modified formulary. Trained to obedience, influenced most of all by the direction of
their own spiritual Father, Singlin, they put their
names to the hated paper.

All of them made the "distinct exceptions" suggested by Arnauld. Jacqueline and her sympathizing friend, the prioress, added to these "a strong
protest in order to clear their consciences in some
degree." Yet, notwithstanding this, remorse and
grief so overcame these noble women that, the next
day, both of them were taken seriously ill. For
nearly three months they lingered. Doubtless the
autumn chill and dampness of the valley had something to do with their condition. But Jacqueline
said of herself that she was "a victim of the formulary." "I speak in the agony of a grief which *I feel
certain will kill me*," she had said in her "Letter on
the Formulary," and the clear-headed, conscience-
searching nun was not given to exaggeration. "It
was the woman, not the Christian which sank," says
Vinet, "overwhelmed by the weight of her own
courage."

The prioress, with much difficulty was restored to
health. Jacqueline never rallied. On her birthday—
October 4, 1661, just thirty-three years old—she died.

We have no details of her last days. We only know that neither brother nor sister were with her, that the Mère Angélique was dead and Agnes very feeble and imprisoned at Paris, that she was denied the presence of her beloved Father Singlin. But the Lord remembereth His own, and, doubtless, she was ministered unto according to her need.

" Her life," says Vinet, " is the life of an energetic woman ; her death—that of a woman. She died of grief, because, under the guidance of the great Arnauld, and of the distinguished leaders of Port Royal, she had consented to a transaction deemed proper by them all, but in which the exquisite delicacy of her moral sense detected a slight evasion."

# THOSE LEFT BEHIND.

# XIX.

### THOSE LEFT BEHIND.

THERE was fresh sorrow in the convent now, for "Sœur de Sainte-Euphémie" was greatly beloved. A touching and beautiful letter was written by the abbess to Pascal, informing him of their common loss.

D'Andilly's daughter, Angélique de St. Jean, a very lovely and talented woman, just Jacqueline Pascal's age, wrote to Madame Perier. Her letter is rather an outcry of sisterly grief than an attempt at consolation.

Good, quiet, unpretending M. Perier came from Paris, hoping to find his sister-in-law still alive. "He seems so grieved," writes Angélique. "I pity him for the sad news I have not yet dared communicate. The Duke of Roannez is also here. I am very glad of that; yet earthly consolation is little worth. Alas! how much I had hoped for, in all our present and future trials, from her whom God has taken away, lest we should lean on her too much."

Father Singlin wrote a tender epistle to his daughters in the Lord, holding up for their imitation the virtues of their beloved sister. In the annals of the convent, Jacqueline is spoken of as, in all respects, "a perfect nun—one whose eminent piety equaled the nobility of her intellect."

The brother and sister were, in death, not long divided. In August, 1662, Blaise Pascal died. His last months were an accumulation of sufferings—disease, penances, and griefs.

His only remark on hearing of Jacqueline's death was, "God give us grace to die as well." "Yet," says Madame Perier simply, "she was assuredly the person whom he loved best in all the world." He endured all trials with a beautiful patience. He was ashamed, he said, of having so much kindness and attention lavished upon him, while so many of Christ's poor had not where to lay their heads.

While the body wore away, the active mind was reaching farther and farther out into its own boundless realm.

In these last years were written those "Pensées" which will live even longer than the "Provincial Letters." They were jotted down on bits of paper and pinned together without classification. "Fragmentary, but grand—they are like some temple portico in the sands of Egypt, ruined before finished, but whose glory will never pass away."* They were intended as parts of a great work on the evidences of the Christian religion, the general plan of which he once sketched in conversation with the Duke of Roannez and other friends.

Once Pascal returned, for a brief season, to mathematical studies. In the course of a few sleepless nights, caused by the agony of tooth-ache, he thought out, merely for the sake of distraction from the pain, a system which came within one step of being the "Differential and Integral Calculus." Tulloch says that if he had pursued this train of thought "it may confidently be presumed that he would have anticipated Leibnitz and Newton in the glory of their great invention." As it was, Pascal's discovery brought him great honors from all the mathematical circles of Europe.

And who first thought of the dray, the wheel-barrow, the *omnibus?*—who but this "miracle of universal genius"? Sainte-Beuve says: "It seems as if every object he looked at gave him a new idea, often a very practical one."

It is almost a relief to have the intimation of a fault in the midst of the many virtues all Pascal's biographers have presented to us. His sister says: "The

---

* Villemain.

13*

extreme vivacity of his mind made him sometimes so impatient that it was hard to satisfy him; yet as soon as he perceived that he had grieved any one by his impatience, he made up for it at once (*incontinent*) by behavior so sweet and by so many kindnesses that he never lost the love of any one by this fault." We may be sure every word of this is true. The beauty of Madame Perier's "Memoirs" is their moderate tone. .Their repressions are more eloquent than any panegyrics. This very fault of impatience brings out an offsetting virtue—humility. "I have always admired the many great points of this man," said an ecclesiastic who visited him shortly before his death, "but I never knew before the grandness of his simplicity. *He is a child.*"

When the end was near, Pascal insisted on leaving his own house to die at his sister's, because he had taken into his own house a family, one of whom was ill of varioloid, and he would not expose his sister to the risk of coming there.*  "He was almost inconsolable" that they would not let him go to a hospital "to die among the poor," and he begged his sister to take into her house some poor sick person who should receive the same attentions as himself. This would

---

* Madame Perier's residence at that time was No. 8 Rue Neuve Saint-Etienne.  Entering the court, at the right of the *porte cochère,* you find a little isolated pavilion. There, in a room which has two grated windows opening on the street, Pascal died.

have been done if they had succeeded in finding a patient in condition to be moved.

He continued his austerities to the last, and "restrained, even in his dying hours, expressions of tenderness toward those whom he loved."

"Mistaken—misled by a pernicious asceticism." Most truly so, we think. Yet, some men's mistakes are better than other men's wisdom.

That patient elder sister, Gilberte, had, indeed, many griefs to bear. Ten years after her brother, her husband died, and she was then plunged into a sea of pecuniary troubles. Two of her sons died not long afterward. In 1687, at the age of sixty-eight, she herself went to her rest. She was buried in the church of Saint-Etienne du Mont, by her brother's side. Both tombstones may be seen there to-day.

Margaret Perier, the heroine of the miracle, lived to be eighty-seven years old. She did the world good service by collecting the papers of her celebrated uncle and aunt and writing the memoirs of her family. "All my relatives and brethren have died in God's service and in the love of His truth," she says at the close of those "Memoirs." "I am left alone. God forbid that I should ever think of renouncing either!" That she did not renounce either is shown by the following memoranda made by some friend after her death:

"Mad^elle Perier made, at different times, long

sojourns in Paris, where she was the admiration of literary and the consolation of religious people. She had many acquaintances and a great number of friends of both sexes. . . . . She left Paris altogether in 1695, after the death of her sister, and went to live with her brother, then dean of St. Peter's (at Clermont). At first she remained at *Bienassis*, which is the most beautiful country-seat in the environs of Clermont, but she would never allow the smallest party of pleasure to assemble there.

"She had a carriage in which to ride in and out of town, but, after a while, gave up both house and equipage, and finding that the Great Hospital was in want of a superintendent, offered her own services to the directors. They were accepted, and she separated herself from her brother in order to live at the hospital, where, however, her health, which was much impaired, did not permit her to make a long stay. Her brother was now canon of the cathedral. They bought a house in its neighborhood, and they lived there in a very simple manner. She remained there after his death.

"Mad^elle^ Perier was always dressed in black, of the commonest material. Her furniture was perfectly plain. Her only domestics were a valet, who took care of the country property, and two or three maids, who, like their mistress, lived a religious life. They did not wear veils, but little white hoods. One of them, who survived her, had been in her service fifty years.

"Some years before her death, Mad^{elle} Perier lost the use of her limbs, and this compelled her to remain within doors except on festival days and Sundays, when she was carried to the cathedral in a chair. She passed most of her days on a couch, and occupied herself with prayer and reading. Her visitors were always charmed with her conversation. Her mind and memory, which was excellent, endured to the very last. By her will she made the poor, in the General Hospital of Clermont, her legatees."

You do not wish to lay down the book till we have taken a final glance at Port Royal?

Pascal was right. No compromises would avail. *They could not save Port Royal.* It was not the signing of a paper that the Jesuits wanted. It was the giving up of a principle, and these women would not give that up. "You refuse to *yield your consciences* to your superiors. What signifies it that you *are* holy and virtuous?" said the archbishop when he came "in full pontificals, with a terrible countenance," to inspect Port Royal de Paris. "He forbade them to approach the altar as wholly unworthy, contumacious, and mutinous," and he warned them to expect his return at an early day, "to denounce a signal punishment which should make them tremble."

He kept his promise. A rumor (all too true)

reached them one night that the abbess and "all the principal officers and nuns" were to be imprisoned in separate prisons or in Jesuit convents.

The next morning "the great gates of the monastery being opened, the archbishop's state-coach, with others containing his officers, silver-cross bearers, and ecclesiastics, and *eight empty coaches*, with twenty constables with staves, and eighty soldiers fully armed, entered and arranged themselves around the court, with loaded fire-arms and fixed bayonets."

"Oh, *ma Mère*," whispered one of the nuns to Mother Agnes, "is it possible that we, such unworthy disciples, should be sent for with a 'band of men with swords, and staves, and chief priests,' just like the Lord himself?"

"Guards were placed at the doors; and the archbishop alighted from his coach in full state, with his great silver gilt cross borne before him, his mitre on his head, and his train borne by numerous ecclesiastics.

"As he alighted, M. d'Andilly, bareheaded, his hair white as silver, threw himself at the archbishop's feet. He had in that monastery six daughters and had had as many sisters, two of whom yet lived. And in the grave-yard of that monastery were the remains of his mother and his grandmother, both of whom had died exemplary nuns of Port Royal, and one of whom had bestowed on it that very house. He uttered not a word, but tears betrayed what he felt on seeing the hour come when they were, for their constancy in the truth, to be torn from that very house their munificence had bestowed; and to be immured separately in prisons, destitute of everything."

The threat was fully carried out. The Mère Agnes was imprisoned, the last sacraments were refused her when she was believed to be dying, and she was threatened that her dead body should be thrown out unburied. But she recovered, and, after ten months, was sent back to Port Royal *des Champs*, where she died at the age of seventy-eight.

Very thrilling are many of the stories of these days given us in the "Lives of the Nuns of Port Royal." Gertrude de Valois is one of the noblest instances of patient suffering for righteousness' sake. Wealth and honor she gladly left behind, and chose imprisonment, torture, want, even to the verge of starvation, for her earthly portion. She was threatened with burial in unconsecrated ground if she refused, to the last, compliance with the demands of her persecutors. "Sire," she answered undauntedly to the archbishop, "I do not think you can bury me in a spot where my Lord can not find me and raise me up again at the last day."

Port Royal *des Champs* was deprived, like its sister community, of its officers and principal nuns, and, after going through a few brief attempts at "pacification," through the influence of the Duchesse de Lon-gueville, was left, apparently, to die out. Various schemes were proposed by friends of the nuns. At one time the Duke of Roannez offered to buy an island in the St. Lawrence for them and bear the expense of their removal to America. Should we ever have known or guessed their virtues if they had come thus to our doors?

Fifty years after Angélique's death, we are told, there were still twenty-two nuns left at Port Royal *des Champs.* "They were old and feeble women; bedridden, paralytic, dying." They had lived many years shut up in the convent, without confessor, without priest, without sacraments.

Madame de Maintenon made sport of these old women, and urged by her and his Jesuit priests, *le grand monarque,* Louis Fourteenth, decided to disperse them, and forever blot out Port Royal.

In 1709, an officer with three hundred soldiers appeared in the quiet, almost deserted · valley. He seated himself on the throne of the abbess and ordered the trembling, but stout-hearted old ladies to be ready within ten minutes to leave their home. They were to be exiled one by one to different convents. The prioress, with respectful dignity, asked if they might not be allowed to go two by two, as many of them were too infirm to be without attendants. This was refused. Most of them were between seventy and eighty years old; the eldest was eighty-six, the youngest over fifty. "Some died on their journey; others as soon as they reached their destination." They were imprisoned in cells without light or fire; they were deprived of sacraments, and, in some cases, their dying hands were guided to sign that hated, un-modified "Formulary," which no persecution had been able to make them sign.

Was not this enough? No. The convent itself, the farm-house of the recluses, the church, and the grave-yard must suffer. The buildings were razed, one after another, to their foundations. Then "a band of workmen, prepared for their task by drink, broke open the graves of recluses and nuns, tore the bodies from the graves, threw them together in heaps, and allowed the dogs to feed on them. The remains were heaped up in carts and conveyed to a large pit, into which they were cast."

Thus was this heresy crushed out! Thus ended, to human view, the lives and efforts of some of the most gifted as well as the holiest children of the Catholic Church of the seventeenth century. Thus did this diseased and weakening body cut off its healthiest member!

But exiled from that church's altars, denied the consolations of her sacraments, condemned to die in that spiritual penury which was to them so much worse than any other want, these fainting souls found, we believe, at last, that righteousness for which they hungered. They found it in no earthly temples, but in that Church above where creeds are lost in Truth.

They sowed in tears; they doubtless reap in joy. Nor can such seed be without a harvest for us in these ends of the world. Such lives can not have been lived in vain. Such characters are an immortal force for good. Jacqueline Pascal, from her far-off, dishonored grave, still speaks to us a lesson of courage, fidelity, and faith.

# FRAGMENTS GATHERED UP.

# XX.

## FRAGMENTS GATHERED UP.

THERE may be readers who will like to supplement our story with a few further illustrations of its characters.

For such, these fragments have been gathered, and let them feel assured that there is much more of equal interest in the great mass from which these are taken.

### I.

In the history of certain races there may occur an illustrious moment, a unique moment, in which the type of that race, after long elaboration, attains its distinct degree of energy and perfection, sets its distinct and deep imprint on two or three medals, and then is broken forever.  It was so in the case of Blaise and Jacqueline Pascal—two precious vases, shattered by the mighty workings of truth, genius, and feeling within them.—*Vinet.*

### II.

We experience a feeling of more thorough and respectful admiration for her than for him. We doubt whether we have ever met with a character, male or even female, which surpassed Jacqueline's. Had she been a woman endowed with one of those peaceful and innately submissive natures to which the conviction of submission brings repose, we should not say this. But the history of Pascal's sister displays a struggle and a victory of the most arduous kind, and yet complete in its results.—*Vinet.*

### III.

The life of Pascal is worth a hundred sermons, and his acts of humility and self-abasement will do more toward checking the libertinism of the age than dozens of missionaries.—*Bayle.*

### IV.

PASCAL'S CONFESSION OF FAITH.

(Found in his handwriting after his death).

I love poverty because Jesus Christ loved it. I love property because it affords the means of assisting the wretched. I keep faith with all. I do not render evil to those who injure me; but I wish them a condition like mine, in which neither evil nor good is received on the part of man. I try to be just, true, sincere, and faithful to all men; and I have a tenderness of heart for those with whom God has closely united me; and whether I am alone or in the sight of man, I perform all my actions as in the sight of God, who is to judge them and to whom I have devoted them all.

These are my convictions; and I bless every day of my life my Redeemer who has inspired me with them, and who of a man full of weakness, wretchedness, concupiscence, pride, and ambition has made a man exempt from these evils by the force of His grace, to which all the glory is due, for in myself are only wretchedness and error.

### V.

(On the evidences of Christianity).

There is light enough for those whose sincere wish is to see, and darkness enough to confound those of an opposite disposition.—*Thoughts.*

### VI.

I lay it down as a fact, that if all men knew what they say of one another, there would not be four friends in the world. This appears by the quarrels which are sometimes caused by indiscreet reports.—*Thoughts.*

### VII.

Certain authors, speaking of their works, say, "My book, my commentary, my history." It were better to say, " Our book, our history, our commentary;" for generally there is more in it belonging to others than to themselves.—*Thoughts.*

### VIII.

Curiosity is but vanity. Often we wish to know more, only that we may talk about it. People would never traverse the sea if they were never to speak of it; for the mere pleasure of seeing, without the hope of ever telling what they have seen.—*Thoughts.*

### IX.

What advantage is it to us to hear a man saying that he has thrown off the yoke; that he does not think there is any God who watches over his actions; that he considers himself as the sole judge of his conduct, and that he is accountable to none but himself? Does he imagine that we shall hereafter repose special confidence in him, and expect from him consolation, advice, succor, in the exigencies of life? Do such men imagine that it is any matter of delight to us to hear that they hold the soul to be but a little vapor or smoke, and that they can tell us this in an assured and self-sufficient tone of voice? Is this, then, a thing to be said with gayety? Is it not rather a thing to be said with tears, as the saddest thing in the world?—*Thoughts.*

### X.

The style of the Gospels is admirable in many respects, and, amongst others, in this—that there is not
a single invective against the murderers and enemies
of Jesus Christ.—*Thoughts.*

### XI.

The heart has its reasons, which reason can not
understand. . . . . It is the heart which is sensible
of God and not the reason. This, then, is faith : God
sensible to the heart.—*Thoughts.*

### XII.

Discontent is caused by the knowledge of the
vanity of present pleasures and the ignorance of the
vanity of absent pleasures.—*Thoughts.*

### XIII.

"Devotion made Easy." From the ninth Provincial
Letter.

(*Louis de Montalle*, the supposed writer, meets the
worthy Jesuit father).

The moment he perceived me, he came forward
with his eyes fixed on a book which he held in his
hand, and accosted me thus :

"'Would you not be infinitely obliged to any one
who should open to you the gates of Paradise?

14

Would you not give millions of gold to have a key by which you might gain admittance whenever you thought proper?  You need not be at such expense. Here is one — here are a hundred for much less money.' "

At first I was at a loss to know whether the good father was reading or talking to me ; but he soon put the matter beyond doubt by adding :

" These, sir, are the opening words of a fine book written by Father Barry of our Society."

" What book is it ? " asked I.

" Here is its title," he replied : " ' Paradise opened to Philagio in a Hundred Devotions to the Mother of God, easily practiced.' "

" Indeed, father !  And is each of these easy devotions a sufficient passport to heaven ? "

" It is," returned he.  " Listen to what follows : ' The devotions which you will find in this book are so many celestial keys which will open to you the gates of Paradise if you will practice them.' "

" Pray, then, father, do teach me one of the easiest of them."

" They are all easy," he replied ; " for example, ' Saluting her when you meet her image—fervently pronouncing the name of Mary—commissioning the angels to bow to her for us— . . . . the last possessing the additional virtue of securing us the heart of the Virgin.' "

"But, father," said I, "only provided we give her our own in return, I presume?"

"That," he replied, "is not absolutely necessary, when a person is extremely attached to the world."

. . . .

"Why, this is extremely easy work," said I; "and I should really think that nobody will be damned after that."

"Alas!" said the monk, "I see you have no idea of the hardness of some people's hearts. There are some who would never engage to repeat every day even these simple words. . . . . And accordingly it became necessary for Father Barry to provide them with expedients still easier, such as wearing a chaplet night and day on the arm, in the form of a bracelet, or carrying about one's person a rosary, or an image of the Virgin." . . . .

"My dear sir," I observed, "I am fully aware that devotions to the Virgin are a powerful means of salvation, and that the least of them, if flowing from the exercise of faith and charity, as in the case of the saints who have practiced them, are of great merit; but to make persons believe that by practicing these without reforming their wicked lives, they will be converted by them at the hour of death, does appear calculated rather to keep sinners going on in their evil courses, by deluding them with false peace and foolhardy confidence, than to draw them off from sin by genuine conversion."

"What does it matter," replied the monk, "by what road we enter Paradise, provided we do enter it?" (He quotes another Jesuit writer to the same effect).

"Granted," said I; "but the great question is if we will get there at all."

"The Virgin will be answerable for that," returned he. "So says Father Barry." . . . .

"But, father, it might be possible to puzzle you, were one disposed to push the question a little farther. Who, for example, has assured us that the Virgin *will* be answerable in this case?"

"Father Barry will be answerable for her," he replied (quoting).

"But, father, who is to be answerable for Father Barry?"

"How!" cried the monk; "for Father Barry? Is he not a member of our Society?"

XIV.

(In defense of the nuns of Port Royal.   Sixteenth Provincial Letter.)

Cruel, cowardly persecutors! Can, then, the most retired cloisters afford no retreat from your calumnies? You publicly cut off from the Church these consecrated virgins, while they are praying in secret for you and for the whole Church. You calumniate those who have no ears to hear you, no mouth to reply to you. But Jesus Christ, in whom they are now hidden, not to appear till one day together with Him, hears you and answers for them.

## XV.

Violence and Verity.   Twelfth Provincial Letter.)

It is a strange and tedious war when violence attempts to vanquish truth. All the efforts of violence can not weaken truth, and only serve to give it fresh vigor. All the lights of truth can not arrest violence, and only serve to exasperate it. When force meets force, the weaker must succumb to the stronger. When argument is opposed to argument, the solid and the convincing triumphs over the empty and the false. But violence and verity can make no impression on each other.

Let none suppose, however, that the two are therefore equal to each other ; for there is this vast difference between them, that violence has only a certain course to run, limited by the appointment of heaven, which overrules its effects to the glory of the truth which it assails ; whereas verity endures forever, and eventually triumphs over its enemies, being eternal and almighty as God himself.

## XVI.

### *Jacqueline's Letter on the Formulary.*

(She had deemed it her especial duty to mortify
her noble intellect, but she was unable to destroy it;
it still clung to her; and though everything which
she achieved or wrote bears the stamp of mental
superiority, there is nothing comparable in this respect to the Letter on the Formulary. Closeness,
sagacity, vigor of argument, energy of language, every
ingredient of eloquence is there, and stands out in
fine relief from an admirable background of humility.
—*Vinet.*)

The letter is addressed to Angélique de St. Jean,
d'Andilly's daughter. We here give it in full:

"MY VERY DEAR SISTER:—The little notice that
has been taken of our scruples in the matter of the
signature would prevent my recapitulating them at
this time, did the case admit of delay. As it is, I
think I ought to tell you that the difficulties I mentioned in writing to our Mother (Agnes), referred to
the *modified* formulary, the proposed *mandement*, a
copy of which had, by a singular chance, fallen into
our hands.

"We understand very well the pretense that our
signature only binds us to submission to the Church
(that is to say, to silence in matters of fact and be-

lief in matters of faith). Most of us wish, with all our hearts, that the requirement were something worse, for then we could reject it with entire liberty, but now some will feel constrained to accept it, and false prudence or real cowardice will induce others to accept it as an easy means of procuring safety for the conscience and for the person as well.

"For my part, I am persuaded that there is safety neither for body nor for soul in such a course. Truth is the only real liberator, and she makes none free but those who will themselves strike off their fetters—those who confess her so faithfully that she can in turn confess them as the true children of God.

"I can not dissimulate the pain which pierces to the very bottom of my heart when I see those persons to whom God has confided His truth unfaithful to it, and, if I may dare to say so, wanting in the courage to endure suffering, and perhaps death, for truth's sake.

"I know the reverence that is due to the high authorities of the Church; I would willingly die to preserve that reverence inviolate, just as I am ready, by God's help, to die for the confession of my faith. But it seems to me nothing is easier than to unite the two. What is to prevent us—what is to prevent every ecclesiastic, who knows the truth, from answering, when the formulary is presented for signature: 'I know what respect I owe to their lordships the bishops; but my conscience will not permit me to declare that a certain thing is in a book which I have never found there'? And, after that, we may patiently await the result.

"What are we afraid of? Banishment, dispersion. the seizure of property, prison and death, if you will! But is not that our glory, and ought it not to be our joy? Either let us give up the Gospel or follow its principles and esteem ourselves happy in suffering for righteousness' sake.

"But perhaps we may be cast out from the Church! True; and yet who does not know that no one can be really cast out of the Church except by his own will? The spirit of Jesus Christ being the only thing which unites His members to Himself and to each other, we may, indeed, be deprived of the badge of that membership, but we can not be deprived of the membership itself, so long as we preserve the spirit of love, without which no one is a living member of His holy body. Is it not plain, therefore, that so long as we do not erect altar against altar (that is, form or join a schismatic Church), while we continue within the limits of simple remonstrance and meek endurance of persecution, charity will of necessity unite us to the Church by inviolable bonds. It is our enemies alone who will have excommunicated themselves by the divisions they are trying to produce!

"Alas! my dear sister, what joy we ought to feel

if we are permitted to endure some special reproach for Christ's sake! But there is too much pains taken to prevent this, when truth is so disguised that she can scarcely be recognized.

"I admire the ingenuity of the human mind as displayed in the perfection with which this *mandement* is drawn up. It is worthy of a heretic; but for the faithful—for those who know and should sustain the truth—for members of the Catholic Church to stoop to such disguises! I can not believe that such things were ever known in the past ages of the Church, and I pray God that we may all die now rather than be the means of introducing such proceedings into the Church. I find it difficult, indeed, my dear sister, to believe that such wisdom as this comes down from the Father of lights; rather it seems to me a revelation of flesh and blood.

"Forgive me, my dear sister, I beg. I speak in the agony of a grief which I feel certain will kill me, if I have not the consolation of seeing that there are some persons willing to suffer for the truth, and to protest against the weakness of others.

"You know very well that the condemnation of a holy bishop (Jansen) is by no means the only question in debate. His condemnation includes that of the doctrine of our Saviour's grace. If our times are so unfortunate that no one can be found to die for a *righteous man*, yet let it not be said that

14*

there is no one willing to die for righteousness itself!

"Perhaps you will say to me that this does not concern us, because of our own particular formulary which our friends have drawn up for us; I answer two things to that. First, that St. Bernard teaches us that the most insignificant member of the Church not only *may*, but *ought* to cry aloud and spare not when he sees the bishops and pastors in such a state as we see them now. 'Who,' says he, 'can blame me for calling out, though I am but a feeble sheep, if I try to awaken my shepherd when I see him asleep and on the point of being devoured by a wild beast? Even were I so ungrateful as not to do this out of love and gratitude, ought not a sense of my own peril to prompt my utmost efforts to arouse him? For who is to defend me if my shepherd is devoured?' This, as you know, does not refer to our own pastors and friends, for they have as great a horror of disguises as I have; but I speak of the leaders of the Church in general.

"The other thing which I answer, and which I confess to you, my dear sister, is that I have not been able thus far to entirely approve our formulary, even as it now is. I could wish changes in several particulars.

"The first is at the beginning; for it seems hard for persons like us to offer so freely to give an ac-

count of our faith. I would give it, however, but
with a little preamble which should take away the
apparent presumption of such a declaration. The
second point is toward the close, where I would not
mention the decisions of the Holy See. It is true we
do submit to those decisions in matters of faith, but
the vulgar do not discriminate, and it would be
thought that we assented to the condemnation of
Jansen.

"I know very well that the defense of the truth is
not women's business. But when bishops have the
cowardice of women, women should, perhaps, have
the courage of bishops. And, if it is not for us to
*defend* the truth, we can, at least, suffer for it.

"A comparison occurs to me, illustrating my idea
on the decisions of the Holy See. Everybody knows
that the doctrine of the Trinity is one of the principal points of our faith, and Saint Augustine (for instance) would, without doubt, willingly confess and
sanction it; yet, supposing his native country happened to be in possession of a pagan prince who
wished to have the unity of God denied, and a plu-
rality of deities acknowledged, and supposing a certain formulary had been drawn up to this effect, 'I
believe that there are several persons to whom we
may give the name of God and address our prayers,'
do you believe St. Augustine would sign such a
formulary? I do not believe he would, and what is

more, I do not believe he *ought to* if he would. Now what I say of St. Augustine I say also of you and of me, and of the most insignificant persons in the Church. *The feebleness of our influence does not lessen our guilt if we use that influence against the truth.*

"M. de St. Cyran often says that the least truth of religion ought to be defended as jealously as Christ himself. Where is the Christian who would not abhor himself if he had been present in Pilate's council, and when the question of Christ's condemnation arose, had been contented with giving an ambiguous answer? Is not the sin of St. Peter trivial in comparison with such a sin, and yet how St. Peter mourned all his life long over his sin! Follow this comparison to its last results, I beg you. My letter is only too long already.

"This, dear sister, is what I think about the Formulary: I wish it to be clear in all that it contains, and these words or something like them, might, I think, be placed at its head: Ignorant as we are, all that can be expected of us in this signature is a testimony to the sincerity of our faith, and of submission to the Church, to the Pope as its supreme head, and to the Archbishop of Paris, our superior; although we do not think it right that we should be called upon to give an account of our faith as we have never given any occasion for that faith to be called in question; nevertheless, to avoid the suspicions our refusal might occasion, we testify in this public manner that, esteeming nothing so precious as the treasure of a pure faith, we wish to preserve ours at the expense of our lives, if need be; we desire to live and to die humble daughters of the Catholic Church, believing all that she believes, and ready at any time to die for the least of her truths.

"Let us pray God, my dear sister, that He will *strengthen us and make us humble, for humility without strength, and strength without humility, are equally dangerous.* This, more than ever before, is the time for us to remember that the *fearful* have their place with the unbelieving and the abominable.

"If they are contented with the statement I have sketched, well and good. For myself, if the matter is left in my own hands I shall never sign anything stronger. Then let what will come. Poverty, dispersion, prison, death—all these seem to me nothing in comparison with the anguish of my whole future life, if I should be wretched enough to make a league with death instead of profiting by such an opportunity of paying my vows to God.

"It is indifferent to me what *words* are used, provided we give no reason to think that we condemn either the doctrine of the grace of Jesus Christ, or him who has so ably expounded it.

"That is why, in saying ' believe all that the

Church believes,' I have omitted the words 'and condemn all that it condemns.' I believe that this *is not the time to say that*, lest the condemnation of the Church should be confounded with the present decision. · Even as our beloved M. de St. Cyran says, 'Pagans having placed an idol on the spot where a cross once stood, Christians should not go there to worship, lest it should seem as if they were worship-ing the idol.'"

# INDEX.


PAGE

d'AIGUILLON, Duchesse.......... 34, 84
d'Alibrai, M...................... 105
d'Andilly.... .................. 71, 135
 "     and St. Cyran....... 75, 89. 90
d'Andilly's daughter............ 71, 295
Angers.. ...................... 137
Annat, Father.... ............ 257, 260
Anne of Austria....... 87, 156, 257, 280
 "         "      examines the mir-
                    acle .......... 271
 "         "      Jacqueline's poems
                    dedicated to....  20
 "         "      peculiarities....... 10
 "         "      receives appeal from
                    Angélique........ 282
 "         "      Regent........ 85, 166
Anjou, Bishop of ................ 281
Archbishop of Paris........... 271, 283
      "         "   angry.......... 285
      "         "   answer of Ger-
                    trude de Va-
                    lois to....... 303
Armand...................... 35
Arnaulds ...... .......... 135, 138, 197
  "      father of................. 255
Arnauld, Agnes.... 68, 109, 136, 232, 270
  "       "   characteristics...157–159
  "       "   childish characteris-
                tics.......... 137
  "       "   comforts Jacqueline. 211
  "       "   imprisoned at Paris. 291
  "       "   last days ,.......... 303
  "       "   portrait of  .. ..... 134
  "       "    "   by Philip
                de Champagne... 158
  "       "   writes to Jacque-
                line..... 124, 158, 181
  "       "   writes letter to the
                King ........... 282
  "       "   writings of..... 158, 199
Arnauld, Angélique.... 68, 109, 123, 180
  "       "   advice in matter
                of dowry...... 212
  "       "   childish charac-
                teristics.. 136, 137
  "       "   comforts Jacque-
                line.......... 214
  "       "   contrasted with
                Agnes... 156, 157
  "       "   death...... 285, 286
  "       "   leaves Valley of
                Chevreuse.... 281

PAGE

Arnauld, Angélique, letter to Anne
                of Austria... 282
 "         "      sketch of... 134–147
 "         "      takes in benight-
                    ed nuns...... 217
 "         "      view of miracle. 272
 "         "      writes to Jac-
                    queline ...... 124
Arnauld, Anne............ 137, 197, 246
 "      "   as teacher...... 244–246
Arnauld, Antoine (the Great Ar-
                nauld).... 83, 138
 "         "      and the Sorbonne
                    257. 260, 261
 "         "      answers objections.
                    289
 "         "      in favor of signing
                    Formulary. 286, 287
 "         "      Jacqueline's note
                    to .... ....... 289
 "         "      "note of com-
                    mand ".......... 290
Arnauld, Henri................ 137, 281
 "      Madame.................. 152
 "      Madeleine ........... 138, 232
 "      Marie Claire.......... 69, 137
 "      Simon.................. 138
Augustinus, The.................. 54
 "      " contains the Five
                Propositions. 257, 280
 "      " finished........ 58, 59
 "      " What it was....... 61
Auvergne............., ..... 3, 4, 31, 269

BASTILLE...................... 31, 281
Battledore and Shuttlecock..... 58, 249
Bayonne ...................... 56, 57
 "   Bishopric offered to St.
        Cyran.... .......... .. 67
Beau Soleil, Baron and Baroness de. 88
Bellay, M., confirms Jacqueline..... 82
Bernard, St..................... 227, 231
Bible, French translation of.... 228, 281
Bienassis ...................... 125
Body, Pascal's neglect of....... 229–231
Bossuet.... .................... 168, 268

CALCULUS, Differential and Integral. 297
Calvinism or Calvinist....... 42, 61, 138
Capuchin friar, preaches at Port
   Royal .......................... 139
Cid, The.......................... 45

PAGE

Codex claromontanus.............. 6
Condé. Prince of.......... 121, 169, 270
Conti, Prince and Princess of...... 272
Corneille.. ... .......... 44, 45, 268, 273
Cornet, Father. . ............... 257
Champagne, Philip de, painting by. 158
Chapelet Secret, Le................ 158
Charles 1. of England.......... 11, 67
Chevreuse, valley of...... 133. 134, 150
    "    " Angélique leaves
    281
    "    " dampness of. 152, 153
Clermont............. 3, 4, 263, 266
    " Fastings and vigils at. 161–164
    " Hospital.... ........ 300, 301
    " Jacqueline visits.,........ 128
Clûny, Hotel.................... 123

Defretal, Father............. .. 263
De la Bouteillerie.......... .. ..... 81
Descartes................ 25, 99, 100
    " meets Pascal in Paris..... 104
Deslandes.......................... 81
De Wert, John ............... 80
Director of Consciences........... 66
Directress, Jacqueline appointed her
  brother's.... ............ 227, 239
Du Droit,—question............... 260
Du Fait,—question................ 260

Elvira, Countess of Toulouse...... 5
Escobar.. ............. ........... 266
Examination of Jacqueline before
  Grand Vicar.................... 284

Felix, M.... ...................... 271
Five Propositions, The ........ 62, 257
    "    " again marshalled
    out .......... 280
    "    " discussed by Ar-
    nauld and the
    Doctors of the
    Sorbonne .. . 260
Flavie, Sister................. 269, 270
Fontaine .................... 73
Formulary ................... 258
    " Dying nuns made to sign. 305
    " Jacqueline's letter on sign-
    ing the....... 288, 318–326
    " Modified .......... ... 286
    " New ............. 280, 281
Fronde. Wars of the. .............. 169
"Fruit bénit "..................... 156

Galileo. ................... 99
Gassion. ...................... 42
Grand Vicar ............ 271, 283, 284
Granges, Les ... ...... 155, 229, 259
Guemené, Princess........... 86. 87, 271
Guillebert, Pastor.......... 79, 80, 81
    "    " training under.... 113

Hamilton, Sir William (estimate of
  Pascal)........................ 29
Hauranne, Jean du Verger de (St.
  Cyran) ...................... 56

Hautefort, Madame de............ 19
Henrietta of England .. .......... 67
Henry Fourth (of France)...... ... 139
Hippocrates ... .. .. ........... 230
Holy Sacrament, adoration of.. 200, 201
Holy Thorn, miracle of . ..... 268–273
Huguenots .................. 48–50
    " Angélique's aunts........ 139
    " Grandfather of the Ar-
    naulds .... .. .. .. 138
    " resemblance of Jansen-
    ists to . ... 61
Hymn translated by Jacqueline.....178

Jansen, Cornelius, sketch of life. 54–62
    " portrait of................ 134
Jansen's great work (*see* Augustinus).
Jansenism or Jansenist .. 241, 255, 257
    " characterized ........... 256
Jesuits and New Formulary ...... 280
    " and Pascal's experiments.... 101
    " and Provincial letters 262, 263
    " and the Five Propositions.
    257, 258
Jesuits' hatred of St. Cyran.... ... 72
    " influence with government.
    255–257
Jesuits punish Port Royal.. 286, 301–306
    " Schools.... ............... 72

Lancelot. .............. .. ........ 73
Latin Quarter .. ................. 123
Laud, Archbishop .................. 11
Letters of Jacqueline Pascal.... 35, 124,
  173, 190, 205, 215, 221, 223, 224, 229,
  230, 231, 234. 269, 270, 278, 279, 283, 288
Letter on Formulary........... 318–326
Letters, Provincial, (*see* Pascal, Blaise).
Liancourt, Duc de . ........... 259
Longueville, Duchesse de.. 169, 271, 301
Louis XI ................. ...... 7
Louis XIII .................... 10, 85
Louis XIV... ................. 86
    " conscience of............ 280
    " disperses the nuns. ..... 304
    " education of............. 167
Louvain.... ........ ........ 56, 58

Maintenon, Madame de.......... 304
Maitre, Le .. .................... 138
    " Madame Le....... 135, 136, 228
Mandement (modified formula). 286, 289
Marion, M ............. ........ 135
Maternité, La (Hospital)... ... ... 123
Mazarin, Cardinal. 85, 137, 156, 166, 169,
  257, 280
Medici, Cosmo di... ............. 99
Mersenne, Father .................. 100
Molière ........ .............. 268
Mons, M. de (assumed name of Pas-
  cal) ........................... 263
Montalte, Louis de (Pascal's *nom de
  plume*)..... .. .............. 266
Montpensier, Mad'selle de. ........ 18
Morangis, M. and Madame de...... 18

| | PAGE |
|---|---|
| Nicole... ......... ............ | 286 |
| Novice, Jacqueline as ...... ..... | 205 |
| Novices, Duties as sub-mistress of. | 231, 232 |
| " reception of......... ..... | 218 |
| " Sub-mistress of........... | 239 |
| | |
| Pailleur........................... | 25 |
| Palais Royal ..................... | 10 |
| Pascal, Blaise........... ....... .... | 8 |
| " " atmospherical experiments ......... .... | 98-101 |
| " " austerities of.... 242, 244, | 278, 298, 299 |
| " " calculating machine. 42, | 98 |
| " " confession of faith.... | 310 |
| " " conversion of....... | 83-85 |
| " " death of.......... 298, | 299 |
| " " difficulties in regard to dowry.......... | 208-211 |
| " " settlement of difficulties in regard to dowry ......... | 214, 215 |
| " " dray invented by. ... | 297 |
| " " encourages Jacqueline's project..... .. | 117 |
| " " experiments on sound. | 22 |
| " " fault mentioned by sister............ ..... 297, | 298 |
| " " Geometrical investigations...... ....... | 23-25 |
| " " ill-health.. 96, 97, 102, | 103 |
| " " Jacqueline's letter on taking the vow.. | 206-208 |
| " " later mathematical studies................ ...... | 297 |
| " " love for Jacqueline.... | 296 |
| " " mental struggles.. 115, | 116 |
| " " omnibus invented by.. | 297 |
| " " opinion on signing Formulary ...... | 286, 287 |
| " " Pensées ......... ...... | 297 |
| " " " extracts from. | 311-313 |
| " " Provincial letters. | 259-268 |
| " " Provincial letters, extracts from .. | 313-317 |
| " " Provincial letters, origin of .. .. .. | 260, 261 |
| " " remark on Jacqueline's death ..... ......... | 296 |
| " " "Second conversion". | 223-229, 241 |
| " " simplicity of.......... | 298 |
| " " statue in Tour St. Jacques.... ....... | 107 |
| " " system of learning to read ........... | 234-236 |
| " " system of logic .... . | 236 |
| " " theories of education | 73, 236 |
| " " wheelbarrow invented by ..... ......... | 297 |
| " " worldliness. 192, 193, 241, | 242 |
| | |
| Pascal, Etienne............... 7, 16, | 20 |
| " " answers Father Noël. | 101 |
| " " conducts his son's education.... .. 16, | 23-25 |
| " " Councillor of State... | 116 |
| " " death of . ..... | 189 |
| " " flight from Paris.... | 31 |
| " " Intendant of Normandy .. .... .. | 40 |
| " " Jacqueline's letter to. | 173-177 |
| " " opposes Jacqueline's project . ...... .. | 122 |
| " " slips on ice.......... | 81 |
| " " special love for Jacqueline ... 31, 97, | 123 |
| Pensées (see Pascal, Blaise). | |
| " édifiantes, by Jacqueline | 182-185 |
| Perier, Florin...... ............. .... | 43 |
| " " assists in Pascal's experiments......... .. | 107 |
| " " at Jacqueline's death. | 295 |
| " " austerities........... | 223 |
| " " builds country-seat.... | 125 |
| " " conversion of, and wife. | 85 |
| " " helps with Provincial letters ............. | 263 |
| " " joy in miracle ... .. | 271 |
| " " letter from Jacqueline. | 221, 222 |
| Perier, Margaret . ....... 46, 113, | 263 |
| " " miraculous cure of. | 268-271 |
| " " sketch of after-life. | 299-301 |
| Perier, Madame, marriage of ..... | 43 |
| " " lays aside ornaments. ..... | 114 |
| " " position in regard to Jacqueline's dowry. .. 209, | 210 |
| " " sorrows and death. | 299 |
| Poem on miracle, Jacqueline's (estimate of) . ................... | 293 |
| Poems of Jacqueline (published)... | 20 |
| Pope Alexander VII................. | 280 |
| Pope Innocent X .................... | 280 |
| Pope Urban II .................. | 4, 5 |
| Poitiers (St. Cyran, Bishop of) . | 64 |
| Port Royal ....... ... 73, 108, 116, | 123 |
| " " Constitutions of.... 199, | 201 |
| " " distress at ........ . | 169-171 |
| " " endowing ...... ... | 208-211 |
| " " final scenes at des Champs ..... | 304-306 |
| " " final scenes at Paris. | 301-303 |
| " " fruit of . .. ........ | 156 |
| " " Jacqueline enters... | 215-218 |
| " " Jacqueline leaves home for ..... .. .....•.... | 195 |
| " " Jacqueline's reception at ... .. ..... ... 197, | 198 |
| " " life at .. .......... | 133-156 |
| " " popularity of ....... 86, | 271 |

PAGE

Port Royal, probation at........... 205
"        "      receiving a novice at.... 218
"        "      schools for boys...... 72, 73
"        "      schools for girls..... 244-246
"        "      troubles at. 259, 280, 281-283
Potherie, M. de la.................. 270
Prince Henry of Bourbon.... ..... 76
Prize at Rouen.................. . 45
Provincial Letters (*see* Pascal, Blaise)
Puritans.......................... 12
Pûy de Dome, atmospherical experiments on................... .... 6, 108
Pûy de Dome, finding of Codex claromontanus.................. 6

QUEEN of Poland.................. 271

RACINE.... ........ ........... 73, 168
Raymond of Toulouse............. . 5
Recluses ........ .... ...72, 152-154
Reflections—Jacqueline's on death of Christ ........ ..... 172, 182-185
Renti, Marquis de ................ 230
Richelieu—and St. Cyran........ 66-68
"          death of ...... ...... 85
"          imprisons St. Cyran... 74-76
"          pardons Pascal, Père.... 38
"          play acted before. .. . 33-37
"          receives Pascal children 20
"          speculations. ..... ... 16, 30
"          wars against Huguenots. 10
Roannez, Duc de.. .. .... 242, 295, 304
"          Mdelle de.............. 242
Roberval....................... 25, 105
Rochelle .......................... 139
Rocroy............................ 121
Rouen .............. 39, 43, 44, 79, 80
Rouville......... ..... ......... 79
Ruel, play-acting at............ ..... 35
Rules, Jacqueline Pascal's, for government of children.......... 246-252

SACI, de ............ 73, 228, 230, 281
Saintot, Madame de ............. 17, 37
Serenade, by Jacqueline........... 47
Séricourt, de   .. ............... 71
Sevigné, Madame de............. .. 133
"          Marquis de.............. 271
Singlin, Père  .. ............. ..
"          "      advice as to signature of Formulary ...... 288
"          "      does not approve of Pascal's mirth. .... 264
"          "      course in matter of dowry......... .. 212
"          "      guidance of Pascal. 224-228
"          "      judgment of Jacqueline's "vocation".. 117

PAGE

Singlin, Père, letter after Jacqueline's death........ 296
"          "      opinion on writing poetry............ 180
Skepticism does not attack Pascal.. 84
Small-pox, Jacqueline suffers from. 31-33
"          lines on recovery...... 32
Sonnet, Devotional................ 47
Sorbonne.................. 103, 123, 257
"Spiritual regimen "........ ...... 230
Stanzas thanking God for gift of verse ........ ................. 21
Stanzas on recovery from small-pox. 32
St. Ange, Madame de  ........ .... 87
St. Augustine, studied by the two friends .... .................. 57, 58
St. Augustine, St. Cyran reading... 74
St. Augustine, "mystic tower",.... 125
St. Cyr, Convent of ........... 135, 156
St. Cyran, Abbé de.......... ... 65-76
"          anecdotes of.......... 69-72
"          illness and death...... 90, 91
"          in prison............. 87-89
"          intimacy with Jansen. 56-60
"          portrait of.............. 134
"          released.............. 85
"          sayings of.......... 221, 222
St. Etienne du Mont, tomb of Pascal and sister .................. 209
St. Francis de Sales....... 138, 144, 162
St. Jacques, Tour de.......... 107, 108
"          Faubourg de...... 152, 217
St. Lawrence, river............... 304
St. Germain, verse-making at .... 18-20
St. Sulpice, Duc de Liancourt confesses at.. ......... ........... . 259
System of learning to read, Pascal's ......... ........... 234, 235
System of logic, Pascal's ......... 235

TISCHENDORF....................... 6
Torricelli........................ 99, 100
Tuilleries.......................... 169

VACUUM, theory of ................ 98
Valois, Gertrude de (answer to Archbishop)........ .. .............. 303
Versailles ....................... 134
Verses recited to Richelieu ....... 35
Verses of Jacqueline... 4, 21, 32, 47, 48, 119, 179
Verses written for the Queen.... 18, 19
Vincennes....................... 74, 79
Voltaire ......................... 269

YPRES, Jansen Bishop of........ .. 58